MY ORC-Y BREAKY HEART

MONSTERVILLE, USA, BOOK 8

AVA ROSS

MY ORC-Y BREAKY HEART

Monsterville, USA 8

Copyright © 2023 Ava Ross

Cover art by Wolfraven Studio

Editing/Proofreading by JA Wren & Owl Eyes Proofs & Edits

*For my parents & family who
always believed I could do this.*

SERIES BY AVA

Mail-Order Brides of Crakair

Brides of Driegon

Fated Mates of the Ferlaern Warriors

Fated Mates of the Xilan Warriors

Holiday with a Cu'zod Warrior

Galaxy Games

Alien Warrior Abandoned

Beastly Alien Boss

Bride of the Fae

A Sci-Fi Holiday Tail

Monsterville, USA

Monster on Board
(co-written with Alana Khan)

A Monster Worth Fighting For
(Monster Between the Sheets)

Love at First Orc

Third Galaxy on the Left

Monster Mate Hunt

You can find her books on Amazon.

MY ORC-Y BREAKY HEART

**Is my hot orc neighbor my crush
or is he actually my soulmate?**

My hunky orc neighbor, Vrok, who I'd love to get to know better, keeps ignoring me. But when he overhears me reading the draft of my steamy romance novel out loud, he tells me he has ideas to make the male point of view better.

Yeah, sure.

One thing leads to another, and soon we're not only working on dialogue, but we're also acting out some of the hotter scenes.

Somewhere between Chapter Fifteen and a troll roller coaster ride, we start falling for each other. Then mate bond symbols appear on our wrists.

Now we can't tell if what we're feeling is real or not. If we break the bond, will we still be in love?

My Orc-y Breaky Heart, Book 8 in the Monsterville, USA Series, is a spicy monster romcom. Each book is stand-alone and best if read in order (see below). Expect romantic hijinks with monsters, heat, and a happily ever after.

Check out the entire Monsterville world!
Candy for my Orc Boss
Orc Me Baby One More Time
Gargoyles Just Want to Have Fun
Don't Go Knotting My Heart
Whose Bed Have Your Claws Been Under?
Uptown Ogre
Oops, I Elf'd it Again
My Orc-y Breaky Heart
Hold Me Closer, Fiery Phoenix
Who Let the Demon Out?

CHAPTER I

VROK

I stepped out into my backyard to let my dragonette pet, Merith, do his thing in the grass—which was better than doing it mid-flight where it more often than not plopped on my head.

After placing him on the lawn that needed mowing, I sat on my back steps. My small, dragon-like creature hopped around eating bugs. Sunlight gleamed off his golden scales, and it didn't take more than him shooting me a dragon-y grin for my heart to melt, just like it had when I picked him out of the litter.

"Yes, you're my true love, the only one I'll ever crave," a woman's voice said nearby with so much passion it made my pulse come to a jarring halt.

Swallowing hard, I glanced toward the tall wooden fence separating my backyard from the one next door. The house had sold a month or so ago, and my new neighbors had settled in. Since I was busy building my fledgling security business, I hadn't gone over to meet the new owner yet.

"I long for the days when we'll be together always," she said with in a heady voice. "So much. I promise I won't allow him to control me much longer. Soon I'll be free, and we'll be together."

"He will not control you at all," a deeper voice growled. "I'll protect you, my precious one."

Kissing sounds punctuated the air.

I shrunk on my back deck. Since I was one of the biggest orcs in our community, I couldn't completely hide, but jeez. PDA much? Good thing a tall fence separated my backyard and theirs.

Merith cocked his head, staring toward our neighbor's place.

"I'll kill him," the male voice said with a snarl.

My eyes widened. Not long ago, I'd worked for the local police force. I'd left to start a security business, though I didn't investigate murders. Was I about to find myself overhearing a plan to commit a horrendous crime?

"Please, don't risk yourself," she said. "He's not worth it. You could be caught."

"I'm good at hiding things like that," the guy said.

Whoa.

"No." Her voice lifted. "You can't. If he finds me, I'll gather my stuff and escape the city. If I travel far enough, he'll never find me."

Monsterville wasn't quite what I'd call a city, more

like a small town. But who was I to say? It was all about perspective.

"Love me, precious one," she cried. "Love me. Make me forget about him. I don't want him coming between us any longer."

At least they'd moved on from plotting murder.

There was no escaping the conversation until Merith finished on the lawn. I waved my claws toward him, hoping he'd get the message and do his thing so I could slink back inside. There was no way I wanted to sit out here while they did something sexual.

Moans and kissing sounds swept over the fence.

Take it inside, folks?

"Our love will stand the test of time," the guy said, and my heart pinched.

You'd think I'd be over my longing for love and romance by now. My ex had ripped my heart out by the roots when she left me. Why would I want to sow a new seed?

"You're my passion," he said. "My only reason for existence."

Clichéd, but who was I to comment? The only serious relationship I'd had crashed and burned to ashes a few months ago. If I had my say, I'd never open my heart to anyone other than friends, family, and pets again.

Moans and groans echoed from my neighbor's yard, telling me the guy's words were a success. Maybe if I'd laid it on thick like that, Margie wouldn't have ditched me while we were planning our wedding.

"Complete me, love," the woman said. "Show me how much I mean to you."

The woman's voice should not spark need inside me. She wasn't speaking to me.

"I have no intention of doing anything else," the guy said. "First, I'll strip your clothing from your body and lick you until you scream."

Hell, no, I didn't want to listen to this.

My cock should not twitch. Ugh. Neighbor porn in action.

"Hurry up, Merith," I said softly, but my infernal pet kept clawing at the ground, seeking bugs.

Hopefully, I could retreat inside before anything too hot happened because there was no way I'd sit around listening to something like that.

Bangs rang out as if someone was dragging a chair across a deck. Shit, they were going to do it out in the open and during broad daylight? Their yard was fenced, but the homes in this area were pretty much built on top of each other.

Rising, I crept toward Merith.

Spying me approaching, he took flight. After what I swore was a conniving look thrown my way, he swooped up and over the fence, disappearing into my neighbor's backyard.

A yelp rang out.

Now I'd done it. Just call Merith a cockblocking neighbor.

Wincing, I strode to the gate connecting the two backyards, making a lot of noise to announce I was coming. The former owners of both places used to be best friends and had the gate installed. I'd intended to put a lock on my side but hadn't found the time. I'd add it to the list of the things I still needed to do at my place.

Once my business was running smoothly, I could slow down and make more time for stuff like that.

I creaked the gate open and paused to give my neighbors time to yank on clothing or cover up.

"I'll just grab Merith and go back inside," I said loudly for the same reason. "Sorry to disturb you folks. I . . . didn't hear a thing." Yeah, sure.

Merith had landed on my neighbor's grass, but instead of seeking a snack, he was hopping toward someone sitting—*alone*—on the back deck. With the sun in my eyes, I couldn't see who it was.

"Come on, Merith," I said. "Let's leave these two alone."

"Two?" a woman said.

I knew that voice. It had haunted my dreams since I met her.

Seyla Anderson, the best friend of my friend, Tylik's new wife.

From the moment I saw her, I'd craved her. She'd made it clear she was interested, and I'd done my best to shut her down. My wounded heart couldn't handle another breakup.

Jealousy I had no right feeling surged inside me, followed by a tinge of disgust. The whole time Seyla made it clear she was interested in me, she was professing her undying love for someone else?

My ex was bad, but not like this. Talk about fickle.

"Two as in you and your . . . *partner*," I said. Husband? If so, it was even worse. Disgust came through in my growl. "You've got some nerve, Seyla."

"What do you mean, Vrok?"

"You know what I mean." I grabbed Merith and lifted him, placing him on my shoulder where he spent most of his waking hours.

Instead of clinging to my shirt as usual, he flapped his wings, taking flight. He soared over to land on Seyla's lifted hand.

She carefully shifted a laptop onto a table beside her lounge chair. "Nice to see you again, Merith," she cooed to my pet.

My dragonette purred and stretched out his neck to rub his face against hers. Her laughter rang out; the sound tickling down my spine.

I shook my head and stomped my big feet. "You . . . you . . . You made a play for me while you're obviously in a relationship," I said. It wasn't my place to let the guy know she was a cheater, but buyer beware and all that. He must've slunk inside the house.

Seyla released another low, husky laugh that made my skin twitch. "You think I'm with someone?"

"I heard him. He wants to lick you."

So did I.

I tried to ignore how gorgeous this female was from her long brown hair shot through with natural golden highlights, to her curvy shape and the tiny dimple in her right cheek. Her brown eyes with really long lashes completed the perfect package.

Still chuckling, she rose and walked toward me with Merith perched on her hand. "I'm alone here."

"You were about to do something with another guy."

Her snort rang out. "You almost sound jealous."

I huffed. "Why should I be?"

She shrugged. "I'd like to think it's because you like me, but you ignored me when I . . . as you say . . . made a play for you." She glanced at her laptop. "There's no one here but me. I was reading my latest book out loud."

"Your book?"

"I'm a romance author. I'll be publishing this one in a few months. I'm doing a solid edit right now. It helps to read it out loud. I find so many mistakes that way."

"Wait, you weren't planning to murder someone?"

She snorted. "Not so far."

"And you weren't about to have wild sex on your back deck with a guy?"

"No one I'm interested in has offered me wild sex yet." Her heated gaze traveled down my frame, and my cock kicked into action. "Are you offering?"

"Of course not," I bellowed.

Her lips twisted. "You could let me down easy."

Flustered, I could barely think, let alone talk. Back to her book. I might be able to discuss that in a reasonable tone of voice.

I was not tempted to rip off my clothing and take her up on her possible offer. Or maybe I was.

"You don't have the guy's words right," I blurted out.

Her hand snapped to her hips, and fury lit up her pretty eyes. "I imagine you think you can do it better."

Oh, I could do *it* better, but she'd never find out.

Before I could hold the words back, they popped from my mouth. "Why don't I help you with the guy's dialogue?"

CHAPTER 2
SEYLA

The orc of my dreams had just made me an offer I couldn't refuse.

"You live next door to me?" I asked, though it was obvious.

He winced. "Yeah."

"Honestly," I said, striding right over to him, "I'm a bit insulted by your offer, though you should know this isn't a final draft. My dialogue will be smoothed out and perfect by the time I'm finished."

He scratched the back of his dark green neck and screwed up his face. "You're sure about that?"

I lifted my chin. Did he see the smile trying to curl up my lips? "I know what my readers like." I didn't need some guy telling me how to make it better, even if the guy was the hot orc I'd crushed on for over a month.

However, I pretty much drooled whenever Vrok sauntered into my orbit. I'd be foolish to tell him to leave and take his offer with him.

"I'd only suggest a few things," he said, clearly back-tracking.

"Tell you what," I said, waving to the other chair on my deck I'd dragged over to put my feet on. "Let's work on a few lines. You can tell me what you'd say to a woman instead. It's a wyvern romance, by the way."

He frowned. "Wyvern, huh?"

"Readers love monster romance." I nibbled on my lower lip, and his gaze focused there.

"Why not an orc, then?"

"I suppose I could change it, though orcs don't have wings."

A scowl rose on his face. "You sound disappointed about that."

"Flying could be fun, right?"

His scowl deepened. "No one needs wings."

"Tell that to my wyvern hero."

"Whatever."

I grinned. "Imagine a hot, steamy wyvern who loves my heroine more than his own life."

"You haven't already, uh . . ."

"What?"

"Nothing," he said quickly.

Actually, I knew where he was going with this. He was wondering if I'd written an orc romance in addition to my wyvern. I was seriously contemplating it.

I did fantasize about Vrok, though I'd held off writing an orc romance so far. When I wrote, it was pure fiction. I saved my fantasies for when I was alone at night and inside my bedroom. I kept hoping they'd come true one day, and the real Vrok would crawl into bed with me.

"I shouldn't help, actually," he said.

"You offered."

"I did not."

I rolled my eyes. "You're saying I imagined it?"

"Well . . . no."

"So sit," I said, waving to the deck chairs. "If you dare."

He frowned. "Why would you need to dare me to sit?"

"Because you run away whenever I come near."

He drew himself up stiffly. "I've done no such thing."

"Then sit."

Grumbling, he climbed onto my deck and dragged one of the lounge chairs as far away from the other as possible. He perched on the edge, glaring my way.

Ha. This was going to be fun.

I urged his cute little dragonette up onto my shoulder, and he clung to my shirt, purring encouragement into my ear—or what I was going to call encouragement. In my fantasy world, he could be a matchmaking dragonette, determined to nudge me and Vrok together.

I wished.

I dragged my lounge chair over until it nestled beside Vrok's.

His frown deepened. "You don't need to come that close."

"I don't want to talk loudly. If you overheard, the nice old lady on the other side might as well. She'll be scandalized and will call Sheriff Venom to report me for watching porn or something like that."

"You said it's *romance*, not porn."

"I'm surprised you know the difference."

"Some guys might not, but I do."

Interesting.

Because I didn't want to dislodge Merith, I carefully settled in my chair and placed my laptop on my thighs, squinting at the screen. "Where do you want to start?"

"Are you sure you want my help?" He appeared more stunned that I'd taken him up on his offer than horrified. A good sign.

"I'd love your help." Mostly, I was curious to hear what he'd suggest.

"We could go over some dialogue." Turning, he kicked his feet up on the lounge chair, leaning back. His legs stuck out comically beyond the end of the chair.

"Do they make chairs for orcs?" I asked. I'd look online tonight. If he was going to hang out with me—swoon!—I wanted him to be comfortable. While I was at it, I'd see if they made orc-sized beds. It never hurt to dream.

"Where I grew up, yes."

"Where was that?"

"In an orc village."

"See? You're the perfect one to help me with my monster romance, then." I tilted my laptop screen so I could more easily read. "I'll start at the beginning. Let me give you a little background about the story. In the beginning, they meet online. Or she thinks they do. She actually half falls in love with his mother."

"What?" he barked.

Grinning, I held up my hand. "No worries about that; it all works out in the end. His mother placed a mail-order bride wanted ad, pretending to be her son, and my heroine responds. They email each other back and forth, her thinking it's him the entire time. Then his mom proposes, she agrees, and they're married by proxy. The book starts with her showing up on his back doorstep."

"This doesn't sound very believable."

"It's my story," I growled, though I wasn't truly peeved with him.

He winced. "Okay; I'll deal with it." His chin lifted, and he shot me a look I couldn't define. "What does the guy say when she shows up and explains?"

"Let me get to that part." I scrolled to the end of chapter one and read out loud. "Get lost, woman."

He frowned. "That sounds mean."

"My wyvern is grumpy. Growly. He was wounded by others in the past and he lacks trust."

"Okay." His head tilted. "What does she do?"

"Steps inside his house, of course."

"Why of course?"

"Because her father's a bad guy, and he was going to force her to marry someone to pay off a debt."

"Now *that's* mean."

"Right?"

He grinned. "This sounds like a fun story."

"Thanks." My spine loosened. Finally, I was talking with Vrok. Could something more come from this?

Back off, Seyla, I told myself. *He's helping you with your book, not offering to replace the alien vibrator in your bedroom.*

"Is the guy attracted to your woman?" he asked.

"Her name's Nettie."

He scowled. "Nettie?"

"Do you have a problem with the name?"

"Not really. It's your book."

I sighed. "I like Nettie. The name's not open to discussion."

"Okay." He scrunched his lips together.

Why did they have to appear so kissable? I wondered what tusks would feel like during a kiss, but sadly, I'd probably never find out.

"If you'd like a suggestion . . ." he said.

"Tell me."

"I think instead of telling her to get lost, he should say something like, who the hell are you? That implies he has no idea who she is, and it's still grumpy."

"That's perfect." And now I was the one who felt stunned. "You're good at this." I quickly changed the last line of the chapter.

His smile came easier.

We went through the next chapter, and while I didn't take all of his suggestions, I used some of them.

Merith leapt off my shoulder and flew over to land on Vrok's.

Vrok stood. "I should go."

"So soon? I wanted to get to the steamy parts."

His eyes widened. "You write sex scenes?"

"Lovely, heated ones," I said proudly. "My readers adore stuff like that."

"Why?"

"Because it gives them what they can't always get from real guys."

"Then those real guys aren't the right ones."

"That's what I've always thought." I sighed because I was sure I'd never experience love like that either.

"If you want, we can act the steamy parts out." I slapped my hand over my mouth the second the words slipped out. "Sorry," I mumbled around my fingers. "I didn't mean it that way. I meant . . . the dialogue in those scenes."

His thick, bushy black eyebrows lifted. A breeze swept through my backyard, lifting his equally black hair. The sun glinted on his green skin.

"You look just like a monster cover model," I said with a heady sigh.

His eyebrows lifted even further, telling me I shouldn't ask him to pose. I could feel my ship sinking to the bottom of the ocean, never to be found again.

Without saying a word, he leapt off my deck—an almost heroic feat since it had been built about five feet above ground level.

He raced through the gate.

It slammed shut behind him.

CHAPTER 3
VROK

I was doing my bookkeeping the next afternoon inside my office when the growl of a lawnmower made me pause.

"Sounds awfully loud for a neighbor mowing their lawn," I told Merith.

My dragonette fluttered his wings and lifted off my shoulder. He soared across the room and passed the windows overlooking my backyard before returning to land on my desk. He skidded across the surface, taking my paperwork along with him.

"While accounting sucks," I said, rising, "I still need to do it." Rounding the desk, I scooped up the papers and returned them to the surface, placing a rock on top of them to hold them down. "You're fidgety. Do you need a snack or something?"

Merith tipped his neck back and shot a tiny blast of flames into the air. Good thing he didn't generate real fire; it just looked like it could burn the place down.

Smoke coiled from his nostrils as his gaze went from me to my window.

The whir of the mower continued.

"I'll take that as a no," I said, returning to my chair and dragging my paperwork closer. "Almost finished. Then we can take a walk or something, okay, little guy?"

Or we could stop by Seyla's and help her with her book.

Actually, I needed to stay away from Seyla. She made my pulse roar and my heart twitch whenever I was around her.

Leaning over my papers, I went through the columns again. I'd just finished one security job—for my friend who'd recently gotten married—and lined up twelve more. Things were going so well; I'd hired two full-time staff. I no longer had to do direct security myself; I could manage others—my goal all along. If things continued like this, I'd have a crew of five or six within a few months.

A clang rang out, and the mower went silent. Hit a rock? Sounded like it. The steady whirs that followed implied the person was trying to crank the engine over again to get it started, without success. Probably flooded it.

Merith took flight again, soaring around the room before diving toward me. He smacked into the back of my head, which wasn't much better than pooping on it.

"Jeez," I said, rubbing the spot. "Do you need to go outside?"

He flew over to the window and landed on the sill, peering into the backyard.

I generally didn't let him out without going with him, but I needed to finish lining up these numbers before calling it quits for the day.

Standing, I walked toward him. "I'll let you out this once, but don't take off. No wooing the lady dragonettes for you tonight." He wouldn't find any nearby even if he went looking. My family bred and raised them, and there were only a few mating pairs in existence. With slow, careful breeding, they hoped to bring the species back to the numbers that populated the orc kingdom ages ago.

When I reached the set of windows, I frowned, staring out into my backyard.

Someone was mowing my lawn, which totally needed doing. I'd been planning to get out there with a weed whacker and mower soon.

The person hauled on the starter cord, but the mower didn't turn over.

She leaned forward, pointing her curvy, gorgeous ass my way.

Seyla.

CHAPTER 4
SEYLA

"What do you think you're doing?" Vrok challenged from behind me.

I'd wondered when he'd figure out what was going on, though I'd hoped to finish his lawn before he discovered I was the one taking care of it.

"Your grass is too tall," I said, turning to face him.

"I was going to trim it."

"When it had gone to seed? That's not good for a lawn, you know."

His gaze slid down my body. "What the hell are you wearing?"

"You like that word."

He sputtered. "Excuse me?"

"Hell. That's the word you suggested my hero use with my heroine."

"I'm not talking about them. Why are you in my backyard?"

I flicked my hand toward my mower. "I'm taking care of your lawn as thanks for your help yesterday."

"I only gave you a few suggestions."

"I still appreciate it. My hero's going to sound much better thanks to you. We should go over more scenes soon."

"I didn't offer to help any further."

"Pretty please?" I pouted and propped my hand on my hip.

His eyes locked on my hand. He'd noticed I was wearing only a bikini. From the shift in the front of his shorts, his body approved.

"I can help you . . . tomorrow," he said. "Not now."

"Well, my mower won't start, so we might as well work on the book." I waved in the general direction of my house. "My laptop is on my deck."

"You flooded the mower."

"That's what I figured. It needs time to settle before it'll start again."

"I'll mow my own lawn," he huffed.

"Alright. I'll find another way to thank you for your help. Maybe I'll weed your front flowerbeds that are sorely overgrown and scruffy."

His growl rumbled in his chest. Very cute, though I imagined that wasn't the effect he was aiming for. "You did enough. I'll take care of everything. I need the exercise."

I skimmed my gaze down his body, noting the ongoing bulge in his pants. If I could turn him on this easily, things weren't going as badly between us as I'd assumed. "I think you look great already."

"You do?"

"Sure." I stepped toward him and linked my arm through his. "Come over to my place for just a few seconds? I'm at a tough part in the story and really need your help."

He allowed me to steer him through the gate and up onto my deck, Merith soaring close behind us. I'd placed the deck chairs close together in anticipation, but again, he dragged one away from mine.

"I thought we could act out this scene," I said. "I'm not sure I have the movements the way they should be."

Merith settled on his shoulder as Vrok narrowed his gaze on my face. "Will it take long?"

Forever, I hoped.

"Probably not," I said. "Actually . . ."

"What?"

I latched onto his arm again and tugged him inside my house.

"Your laptop's outside," he said.

"It's okay; my phone's on the kitchen counter and I've downloaded it there as well. I need your help with a kitchen scene. Would that be alright?"

"Kitchen as in cooking?"

"More or less."

His posture loosened. I didn't sense he was afraid of me, more that he was leery. A little snooping around town revealed he had a pretty tough breakup about six months ago. The woman he was engaged to had ended things abruptly in the middle of arrangements for their wedding.

I wanted to thank her. Invite her to *our* wedding. I just had to convince Vrok to propose.

We passed my new kitty I'd gotten at the animal shelter a month ago.

"That's Sriracha," I said, waving to the fluffy gray tiger. "Watch out. He looks sweet, but he's spicy."

Sriracha looked up, up, up at Vrok, and his bushy tail spiked up over his back. He danced on his toes, slowly approaching Vrok sideways.

Merith soared off Vrok's shoulder and landed on the wooden floor between Vrok and Sriracha.

My cat paused, frowning at Merith.

Merith released a cheep, and, turning, scurried into the living room.

Sriracha gave chase, his claws clicking on the floor.

"Should we intervene?" I asked, worried about Merith. He might be a dragonette, but Sriracha probably saw him as a bird.

We crept over to the living room and peeked inside, finding Merith and Sriracha sitting on the sofa together, staring at the TV projecting the image of fish swimming inside a fish tank.

"I didn't leave the TV on," I said, bemused.

"Merith knows how to work a remote." Vrok shrugged. "I'd say they're friends. You said something about needing help in the kitchen?"

"Yeah, sure." I remained in the doorway. "You're sure they won't hurt each other? When I said Sriracha's spicy,

I meant it." Lifting my arm, I showed Vrok the scratches I'd received when I brushed my kitty last night.

"Those look sore." Vrok traced his finger down one of the marks, which made my skin tingle rather than cause pain.

"They're getting better." With one last look at my cat, hoping he saw my look to mean *behave*, I walked to the kitchen.

Vrok followed me around the island to the area between it and the counter. "What sort of cooking scene did you write in your book?"

"Well, she's getting things out of the fridge," I said. "Let's act it out." Like my character, I open the fridge, lean forward, and start taking out vegetables, placing them on the counter. Unlike in my book, I wiggle my ass.

Vrok hissed.

"In the book," I said. "He gets turned on by her rooting around in his fridge." Turning with the lettuce in my hands, just like my heroine, I faced him. "He tugs her close and lifts her up onto the counter."

He gazed that way. "You put vegetables there. Your ass will crush them."

I rolled my eyes. "Romance, Vrok. Think romance. What sort of romantic thing could a guy do if the vegetables were on the counter, and he wanted to put her there?"

"I suppose he could sweep them off with his arm. That would be dramatic. I don't know if anyone would see damaging vegetables as romantic, however."

"I would."

"I guess so." His head tilted, and his gaze remained focused on my breasts stuffed into the top of my bikini.

"Maybe it'll feel more romantic if you act it out?" I said. "I'm not quite sure how it would go, and I welcome any suggestions."

"Alright." He swallowed hard, and his arm raked across the counter, sending my veggies flying. "What next?"

"What do you think? He's really hot for her."

"You said he's a wyvern, *not an orc*, but I assume they differ in size? You're so much smaller than me."

"I think their height difference is about the same as ours." Exactly, actually.

"And he wants to kiss her?" Vrok asked, scratching the back of his neck.

"Definitely." I was getting heated by our conversation, and from the twitch in Vrok's pants, so was he.

"He'd do this." Vrok latched onto my waist and lifted me effortlessly onto the counter. This put us almost at eye level.

"Do you think this is close enough to kiss?" I asked, watching his face.

His attention had returned to my boobs, which wasn't a bad thing. From research, I knew it took stimulation for nipples to harden, but mine hadn't gotten the memo. They were thrusting themselves against the front of my bathing suit top, eager for whatever might come next.

"I could lean close to see how a kiss might work with you in this position," he said.

"Only if you feel comfortable." Truly, I wasn't out to seduce him against his will. I wanted him very much willing.

"I can handle it." He leaned close. "You smell good, Seyla."

"Thank you."

"Like clipped grass."

Not quite the effect I was aiming for, but if grass was good, I'd take it. "I was mowing."

"Yes, mowing." He frowned, his eyes going from my lips to my eyes, then back again.

"In my story, she grabs onto his horns," I said. "He likes it when she does that."

"I imagine he does."

"Would you like that?"

"I don't know. No one has tried it before."

"I guess it would be like . . ." I carefully lifted my hands until they hovered over his horns. "Alright to touch?"

Biting down hard on his upper lip with his tusks, he nodded.

"Like this." When I smoothed my fingertips across his glorious green horns, he growled.

His arm went around me, and he tugged me fully against him.

Forgetting my book, I wrapped my legs around him.

His mouth captured mine.

CHAPTER 5
VROK

I was kissing Seyla, and it was the best kiss I'd experienced in my life. Each glide of her fingers across my horns sent shock waves to my cock.

It thrust upward, demanding I let it out to seek her hot core.

She moaned, her lips parting.

I thrust my tongue inside, savoring her heat.

She ground herself against my abs, and even a jet plane crashing into the building wouldn't wrench us apart.

When I slid my fingers up her side, pausing below her breast, she thrust it into my hand.

Feeling her ripe bud through the fabric made me come undone.

I wrenched my mouth off hers. "Say no."

She shook her head, pinching her lips together.

"If you don't say no, I'm going to do more," I snarled.

"Do it."

That was all it took. I slid my fingers across her naked belly and cupped her breast through the skimpy fabric of her top. My cock was on fire. *I* was on fire.

A flick of the claws on my other hand, and I'd sliced through the crotch of her bathing suit, exposing her to me. I leaned her back and crouched, closing my eyes as I took in her heady scent.

I licked her, and a moan jerked from her throat. She lay back farther, her back hitting the upper cabinet, and wiggled her hips toward me until she could smack her thighs onto my shoulders.

Her seam glistened with desire.

Forget books and acting anything out; this was real.

"If I was a guy hoping to seduce you, Seyla," I said. "I'd do this." I plunged my tongue inside her, driving it as far as it would go, then twirled it as I pulled it back out.

She bucked beneath me before stilling. "If I was . . ." She gulped, and I loved that she was struggling for control. "If I was the heroine in my book and you did that, I'd do this." She latched onto my horns and milked them.

Heat blasted through me, centering in my cock. It had never been this hard, this in need.

"And I'd do this," I said. I licked up to her clit and sucked it into my mouth, teasing it between my tusk and my upper lip.

"I'd lose control," she said in a thready voice.

Lifting my head, I shook my finger at her. "None of that. If you're acting this out, Seyla," I said patiently, "you need to show it, not tell it."

"Do it again, then, and I'll try to give you the response you're looking for."

"Oh, you will. You will." I wasn't sure how I knew this, but it was as certain as the green color of my skin. "Enough talking."

I sucked her clit into my mouth and swirled my tongue across it over and over while she moaned and jerked beneath me. I loved that I could make her go wild, that I could give her this much pleasure.

She clung to my horns, yanking on them, almost dislodging my mouth. My grin slipped in there somewhere. Feeling her reaction made me incredibly happy. I hadn't felt this good in a very long time.

I released her clit and lifted my head so I could watch her expressive face. Holding up my hand, I retracted one claw after the other until only my thick fingertips remained.

"Is it finger fucking time, fictitious female?" I asked.

"No more talking, didn't you say?"

"You're too impertinent. This shows me I'm not working you hard enough."

"*Show*, Vrok. Don't tell."

I sucked on her clit again and slid one of my fingers into her welcoming wetness. Her sweet G-spot was right there, calling out to me, so I glided the pad of my finger across it. When I pulled my finger out, I added another, pumping them while licking her clit.

She wrenched her upper body across the counter to lay flat and rocked her hips up to meet my fingers. Her keening cries echoed around us, the most amazing sound I'd ever heard.

Something crashed, falling into the sink, but I didn't stop. Hell, no. I moved my fingers faster, driving them deeper, marveling at how wet and hot she was, how she sucked on my hand and made me crave her more than anything.

Her clit tightened. Her body started to shake. She wrenched on my horns, which made me half-grin. I never left her clit, though, and when my nibbles grew rougher, she shrieked and gave way. I loved how her orgasm consumed her, how she cried out and shuddered, how her passage sucked and jerked on my fingers.

When she finally stilled, I slowed my fingers, still moving them in a lazy swirl.

I gave her clit one last lick, then looked up at her and grinned. "Should we work on your next chapter?"

My grin remained until I noted the marks encircling my wrists.

CHAPTER 6

SEYLA

Crushing on Vrok without even a hint of returned interest on his part had made me feel down.

I slid off the counter, and my shaky legs could barely support me.

As if a shutter had dropped over Vrok's face, he scowled. "I need to get Merith and leave."

On cue, his dragonette swooped into the kitchen, Sriracha scampering behind. Sriracha leaped up onto the island, something I wished he wouldn't do. Lifting him, I placed him on the floor.

He jumped back up onto the island. He laid down and blinked at me as if to say, *you can take me off all you want, but I rule this house, not you.*

The severed underside of my bathing suit bottom dangled between my thighs, but I wasn't complaining that he'd cut it. I'd just had the best orgasm in years, and I wanted more. But it appeared Vrok had regrets already.

Merith left Vrok, soaring over to land on my arm

resting on the counter behind me. I lifted him and gave him some pats while he purred before urging him to return to Vrok. "Go on, little guy. It's time to leave. Come visit me again, though, okay? You can leave the grumpy orc at home."

"I'm not grumpy," Vrok said with a snarl.

My laugh burst out. "You keep telling yourself that." I cooed at Merith. "He also suddenly hates me, so if you come back to visit, do it when he's not looking."

"I don't hate you," Vrok snapped.

"Dislike, then."

"I don't dislike you, either."

I propped my free hand on my hip. "Are you saying you *do* like me?"

"I'd never say that."

"Because you don't. As I said, you hate me."

He sighed. "I like you well enough."

"Well enough?" It was all I could do not to storm over to him, poke his chest, and ask how much he liked me when he was licking me out. "You're laying it on awfully thick there, Vrok," I said. "If you're not careful, I'll take your kindness as encouragement and climb all over you."

He sucked in a breath, and his gaze focused on my mouth.

"Is my lipstick smeared?" I wasn't wearing any.

"What do you mean?"

"You're staring at my mouth. I guess that's better than my boobs, though I'll give you time."

His face darkened, and he raked his fingers across his horns. "Come on, Merith. It's time to go home."

"When did you get tattoos?" I asked, noting the swirling patterns etched in his skin, wrapping around his wrists. "They're nice."

"I don't have tattoos."

"I guess you don't have to share if you don't want to, but what are these?" I tapped one of them, and sparks flared beneath his skin. Holding up my hands, I backed away. "They're alive."

He lifted his arms, staring down at them. "They're . . . They're . . . They're nothing." He snatched Merith from me and turned, racing from my house.

With a sigh, I followed, locking the door and watching as he fled through the opening in the fence, shutting it behind him.

Sriracha wound around my legs, and I stooped down and picked him up, draping him across my shoulder. "What do you think, spicy boy? Does Vrok like me or not?"

Sriracha just purred.

In need of a treat, I drove to Rylee's bakery the next morning. Inside, I rushed around the counter and hugged my best friend, Kate, who worked there.

"Great to see you," she said with a smile. "How are things?"

I shrugged. "Okay."

Her face fell. Stepping away from me, she opened one of the cases, selected a chocolate cupcake with peanut butter frosting—my favorite—and placed it on a small plate. She grabbed two plastic forks from a tray, then took my arm and dragged me into the back of the shop, calling out to Rylee. "Be right back. Intervention in progress."

Rylee chuckled and winked at me. "Good luck!"

I rolled my eyes and went with my friend. We passed through the kitchen where a yeti and an ogre worked on various baked goods. The sweet smell of sugar coated my sinuses and made my belly rumble.

We went through the back door, stepping out onto a small deck holding a table where staff often ate their lunch.

Kate placed the cupcake in the middle of the small table and pushed me into a seat. "Tell me all about it."

"Yes, Mom," I said, and we chuckled. Not too long ago, when she was suddenly engaged to an elf, Tylik, and falling fast for him, I was the one giving her guidance. She'd called me 'Mom' then.

"What did he do?" she asked, taking the seat opposite me and handing me a fork. "Do you want me to ask Tylik for a spell? We can make Vrok disappear."

Her husband owned an apothecary where he dispensed various ingredients to perform magic.

A few years ago, monsters stepped out of the woodwork, so to speak, and into human society. Treaties were formed, and in the case of elves, magical rules were laid down. They were allowed to cast simple spells, but nothing stronger than that.

Monsters had been living parallel lives to humans, so

many fit in seamlessly. Others maintained their own customs and rules, however, and they were respected by the humans.

Many of the monsters had settled in this town that used to be called Blustery Hills. Everyone now called it Monsterville. Enormous, snow-tipped mountains and endless forests surrounded the town, and many of the monsters still lived within the woods, coming into town for supplies or to go out to dinner.

Rylee and her orc husband had moved here from Screaming Woods, a town where a professor accidentally turned humans into monsters. Her husband was an orc like Vrok.

Kate cut the cupcake in half, stabbed a fork into one of the sides, and nudged it my way. "Eat. Talk. Share."

I grinned, though it made my face ache. "I spent last night feeling sad."

Kate's answering smile fled. "Aw, I'm sorry. What happened?"

"Everything seemed to be going okay, but now it's turned sour all over again."

"I assume you're referring to Vrok."

"My cute orc neighbor who wants me but doesn't want me."

"Neighbor?" she barked. "When did that happen?"

"A month ago when I moved in but made no effort to get out and introduce myself. He was there all along, but we've recently connected." I ate a bite of cupcake and told her what had happened, though I skimmed over him eating me out in the kitchen. "He left, and despite me going over to his place and knocking on his door, I haven't seen him since."

Kate shook her head. "You two acted out a scene in your book? What an amazing idea."

"I need the help. He's good with dialogue."

"And a few other things, from what you've implied." She ate a bite and licked the peanut butter frosting off the fork.

I sighed. "*So* good."

"You're giving up, then, are you?"

"Would you?"

She chuckled. "With Tylik? Never."

I loved seeing them happy together. Their relationship might've started in an unconventional way with a fake engagement to please his aunt, but they truly loved each other.

"I'm not sure what to do next," I said, eating more cake. Rylee's baked goods must be infused with magic because they tasted amazing.

"You've got more book to act out, don't you?"

"Do you think he'd be willing to help me again?"

"Asking him to give you pointers on your kitchen scene is truly inspired."

"The thing is," I said, "I wasn't faking or doing something to lure him in. Sure, I did some ass wiggling, and I was wearing a bikini so he could see quite a lot with me in that position, but I was just teasing, hoping to get a rise out of him."

"I'm sure *something* was rising." Kate scraped the last of the frosting off the plate and licked it off her fork.

"Ha, maybe."

"If he was doing what you were suggesting, he had a stiffy."

"It doesn't matter. He shuttered, got all snarly, and stalked away."

"There are things you can still do. Finish his lawn."

"He did it during the night," I said. "I watched him out the window."

"You didn't go down?"

"He hates me." I drooped in the chair. Despite the chocolate, I was still sad. "Why bother?"

Kate shook her head slowly. "I can't believe you're giving up this fast."

"What can I do?" I half-wailed.

"He's your next-door neighbor. Surely you can think of something."

"Not really. I mean . . ." I frowned. "Hold on."

Kate grinned. "There's the friend I know and love." She leaned across the table and nudged my arm. "Go get 'em."

CHAPTER 7

VROK

In the eight months I was engaged to Margie, she'd berated me numerous times for not showing the markings that would prove we were fated mates. I'd explained over and over that they weren't common even among orcs, let alone in a relationship between an orc and a human.

"Chastity has them," she'd say with a heavy sigh. "Max loves her more than you do me."

There are times now when I wonder what I'd seen in her, but back then, I'd thought I loved her.

Well, marks had finally appeared on my wrists—and not because of Margie. I was licking Seyla when they appeared.

She was not my fated mate. I didn't want one. And she sure as hell wasn't my orc wife. Didn't want one of those either.

"Fuck," I hissed.

I'd already done this three times, but there was no

harm in trying for a fourth time. I turned the water in the kitchen sink to full blast and ran my wrists underneath the flow. Taking the green scrubber, I ran it across the marks, over and over, hoping they'd fade or disappear completely.

If anything, they blazed darker.

Gulping, I backed away from the sink with my hands lifted as if I was a surgeon prepped to head to the O.R.. I slunk over to stand beside my front door. I peered around the curtain, sure I'd see Seyla standing on the stoop, grinning at me. She'd call out through the door, making up some story about how the couple in her book was going to have sex for the first time—in doggie position, no doubt—and how she and I needed to act it out.

I'd open the door, strip off her clothing, and take her across my kitchen table.

After turning the water off, I fled my kitchen, passing Merith sitting on the back of the couch where he enjoyed roosting.

Inside my office adjacent to the living room, I turned on my computer. It didn't take long on the orc forums to find pages of information about fated mates and the symbols that appear on the mated couple's wrists when they finally found each other.

My symbols weren't exactly the same, but the comments indicated each set of symbols were unique to the couple, that only those two would match.

Did Seyla have them too? I hadn't seen them yesterday, which could mean she wasn't my *real* fated mate.

Or they hadn't appeared yet.

If I remained away from her, they might not, according to the comments on the forum. With enough time and distance, mine might fade. And as long as I stayed away from her forever, I wouldn't crave her any more than I already did.

Someone knocked on the front door.

Shit. It was her here for doggie style. My cock snapped to attention, determined to serve in whatever position she offered.

"Fuck." With my elbows braced on my desk; I cupped my face.

Another knock rang out on my front door.

Had I locked it? I got up and crept to the front hall.

Even now, mating chemicals churned through my veins, making me long for her. On an intellectual level, I understood why. It ensured survival of the species. An orc would enter a full rut and fill his mate with his cum until she was carrying his young.

If it was Seyla outside, I might not be able to resist her.

"I *can* resist her," I hissed.

"Are you in there, Vrok?"

My shoulders sagged with relief. I unlocked the door and let my phoenix friend, Nyxor, inside, while quickly peering out the door but not finding Seyla lurking nearby.

"Are you working?" Nyxor asked, passing me in the entryway and continuing down the hall. His wings fluttered briefly before settling on his back. Dark and with bits of gold and orange, they were the only place my friend had feathers, though they were tiny and lay flat.

Merith shrieked out a welcome as Nyxor settled on the sofa, compressing his wings against the cushions

"When did you get the tats?" Nyxor asked, squinting at my wrists.

"Never."

He shook his head; his dark hair shot through with the same orange and yellow shifting on his shoulders. On anyone but a phoenix, the hair would look odd, but it suited his species. "If you say so."

I sighed and settled in my recliner, though I didn't put up my feet. "They're mating symbols."

"Whoa," Nyxor said. "When did you mate with someone?" He looked around. "I don't see anyone here with you." His green eyes widened, and he shot a look at the ceiling as he rose off the sofa. "Jeez, I'm sorry. You and she were . . . I've interrupted you during this vital orc moment."

"She's not here."

He frowned, dropping back onto the sofa. "Why not? Aren't you two supposed to be . . . well, screwing around a lot to make a bunch of orc babies?"

"Orcs rarely have more than one child at a time."

"You know what I mean. Who's the lucky lady?"

"Seyla is not my fated mate," I insisted.

"Seyla, as in Kate's friend? The one who's been crushing on you forever?"

"She doesn't like me." She just enjoyed my tongue.

On her flesh. And on her breasts, I imagined, though we hadn't tried that yet.

Nyxor shrugged. "From the little I've seen, she does." He shot me a grin. "I'm really happy for you. It's rare for a phoenix to find their fated one. Such an honor."

"She's not my fated mate."

"You can protest all you want, but the symbols prove you're wrong."

"I'm going to stay as far away from her as possible, and the marks will fade. As long as I don't have sex with her, the bond won't tighten."

"So no half-orc babies."

I shouldn't be picturing Seyla holding my child right now. In the image, she looked up at me standing beside her. Her hand reached for mine, and we both stared at the precious infant we'd made together.

"No half anything babies," I snarled.

"Will avoiding her be enough?" Nyxor asked.

"I hope so."

"Why not give into it?" he said. "I would."

"Would you?" I studied my tall, broad-shouldered friend.

"I plan to if I find her."

I had to hand it to him; he was willing to keep trying even after his girlfriend moved out three months ago, telling him she never wanted to see him again.

"How do you plan to find her?" I asked.

"That's why I came to see you. I was thinking of going to Monster Mingle, the new matchmaking service in town, and talking to Grannie Vi and Uncle Bub."

Grannie Vi wasn't his grandmother, and Uncle Bub wasn't his uncle. But was Violet's uncle. She was married to a gargoyle named Goreg. And Grannie Vi was Rylee's grandmother. They were a couple now, and they also lived here in town.

"I'm hoping they can fix me up with someone," Nyxor said. "More than one match if that's what it takes to find the right one."

"Have you looked around town on your own yet?"

"She's around somewhere." He smacked his chest with his fist. "I feel her."

"Or him."

He shrugged. "Right. I think I'm hetero, though, so probably a her." He leaned forward, bracing his big hands on his knees. "Do you think Monster Mingle's the right idea? They can broaden my reach to surrounding towns."

"There's no harm in trying."

"You could come in with me. They have a two-for-one special going on right now."

I snorted. "They don't charge a fee to begin with." They provided the dating service because they loved fixing people up—or in this case, monsters and people up.

"Just a thought," he said.

"I don't want to date anyone."

"You shouldn't let Margie hold you back."

I braced myself for the stab of pain I always got in my chest when her name was mentioned. Surprisingly, I didn't feel much of anything. Perhaps I was finally moving on. "It's more than about her. I'm just not ready to go out with anyone." My mind darted to Seyla, but I dragged it away. "It's hard to trust someone new."

Rising from the sofa, he shrugged. "Margie wasn't the right one."

Again, I thought of Seyla. Again, I shoved her image from my mind.

"If you change your mind, let me know," he said, rounding the sofa and heading for my front door. "I'll make an appointment but set it a week or two away. We could double date."

I snorted. "Do people still do stuff like that?"

"It's a way to keep the date light. If it gets awkward, you chat with your buddy."

"Not so good for her."

"She'd do the same thing. Or she and the other woman would mysteriously need to go to the bathroom at the same time, and before you know it, she's scooting out the front door."

I frowned. "Has that happened outside of a movie?"

"Sadly, yes."

I slapped my friend's shoulder. "Tell you what. If you line up a date through Monster Mingle, let me know. I'll show up and be your friend if you need one."

"Deal."

He left, and I returned to my office where I put in a bid for a job at the mall and studied some figures for another job I was contemplating taking.

Someone knocked on my front door.

Thinking Nyxor might've forgotten something, or it

was UPS delivering the things I'd ordered online, I left my computer and strode through my living room to the front door, tugging it open.

My welcome smile fell fast.

"I baked these for you," Seyla said, holding up a plate full of cookies.

"I don't want them," I barked, trying to shut the door. The symbols on my wrists tingled.

Alert! Alert!

I needed to put space between us before I did something stupid like tug her inside and press her against the wall. Capture her mouth. Her body. Whatever she'd give me.

She wedged her foot inside the opening, and despite my urge to nudge her out of the way and slam the door shut, I didn't want to hurt her.

"I'll just put them on your kitchen counter and leave," she said, bustling inside. "You can nibble on them later."

I wanted to nibble on her.

More than nibble. I might actually take a bite or two.

My cock kicked into action, stating *it* hadn't seen any action in months and that it was more than ready to break my dry spell with Seyla.

Merith, the betrayer, lifted off the back of the sofa and soared over to Seyla, landing on her shoulder.

"Hey, little one," she cooed, stroking his bright gold scales. "At least you're glad to see me."

"You need to leave and take your cookies with you," I snarled.

"Testy, aren't you?" With Merith riding her shoulder like a pirate's parrot, Seyla brushed past me, heading toward my kitchen with her plate in hand. "Maybe you haven't had coffee yet? Let me make some. We can sit and have it with some cookies."

I needed to make her leave before the mating chemicals inside me roared to life. "Go."

She rinsed out the coffeepot and filled it, pouring the water into the top of the unit. "Is your coffee in the cupboard?" Opening one door after another, she found it and carefully measured some into the filter, placing it in the compartment before pressing the button. "While that does its thing, you can explain something to me."

"What?" I perched in the opening to the kitchen, unwilling to approach her.

She held out her arms. "What the hell did you do to my skin?"

Symbols identical to mine encircled her wrists.

CHAPTER 8

SEYLA

"They're nothing," Vrok said, whipping his hands behind his back.

"They weren't there the other day, and if I remember correctly, they're a perfect match to the ones on your wrists." I darted around him and latched onto his hands before he could try to hide from me again. "Look at that." I poked his wrist. "Look at that!"

"It's a temporary issue."

"You mean they'll fade?" I strolled around to stand in front of him again.

For whatever reason, I wasn't panicking about this. No, after seeing the symbols on my wrists while showering this morning, I'd calmly dressed, went downstairs, loaded cookies onto a plate and put plastic wrap over it. I walked to Vrok's front door and knocked.

"Mine match yours." I poked his wrist again, and tingles shot up my finger, pausing to loop around my wrist before shooting up my arm. The markings I'd discovered this morning blazed bright green before fading to a low hum.

My stupid clit started throbbing like a heartbeat. And I had a wild idea if I checked Vrok's pulse, the throbbing would match his rhythm.

"They'll go away if we stay away from each other," he said, backing away from me.

"Why are they there?"

"Have you ever heard of fated mates?"

"Only in sci-fi romance novels."

"Fantasy too, as you've probably discovered while working on your wyvern romance."

"I've written about fated mates, true mates, et cetera in many of my novels. It's a popular trope." Why hadn't I thought of that when I spied the symbols? Maybe because I wasn't a character in a novel! "We can't be fated mates."

He huffed. "Why not?"

"Because you hate me." I stroked Merith still riding on my shoulder, and he started to purr.

"I don't hate you."

"You don't like me very much, though, do you?"

"It's not you," he said.

I shook my head, my lips twisting. "That's what they all say. I'm not even sure what it means." My heart pinched tight. I'd liked him for over a month now, but despite my efforts to make him see me as someone he might like too, he kept shooting me down.

Other than when his fingers were pumping inside me, that is.

The memory pulsed through me, and my breathing picked up. My stupid clit throbbed some more, and my eagerness to feel his fingers again saturated my panties. I leaned toward him. Please let him touch me. Consume me.

"Don't do that," he growled, backing away with his hands lifted.

"Do what?" I wrenched my mind sideways, dragging it out of the warm pool it had fallen into, making it a little easier to think. "I need clarification here. You tend to say general things but avoid giving me a full explanation."

"We activated something that's only supposed to happen with orcs."

"The fated mate thing." Frankly, should I be surprised? No wonder I couldn't stay away from him.

"Yes, but I assure you, it's not permanent."

"It is in my books." I stepped toward him again.

He backed until he ran into the kitchen wall. "As long as we don't have full sex—"

"You mean with penetration?"

His cock was bumping against the front of his pants. And lights kept flickering beneath the symbols on his wrists, mesmerizing me.

"Yes, penetration," he said.

"You're saying as long as we don't fully do it, we won't solidify the bond?"

"Exactly."

"We could still kiss and touch each other. I could

suck you off and you could do the same, all without making this permanent."

"I guess so," he growled, suddenly stalking toward me.

I met him halfway, bumping into him.

He latched onto my arms. "So no penetration, get it?"

"While I do adore the idea of penetration," His penetration in particular. I hadn't had the best experiences with other guys. "I can abstain if I have to."

He lifted me until we were level. "Does it make sense now?"

Barely able to think, I nodded. I took a deep breath, drinking in his scent, and he did the same.

"You're aroused," he said.

"I can't seem to help it."

"It's the bond."

"Are you sure about that? I think it's you, Vrok. Pure you. You turn me on with a single glance."

"You shouldn't say things like that," he grumbled.

"Why not?"

"Because then I can't stop myself from doing this."

Pivoting, he pushed me against the wall.

I wrapped my legs around him as he stepped into me.

He shifted his hips, rubbing his hard, thick length across my crease.

Our height difference was pretty much comical. In order to connect, I stared at his chest while he got a great view of the wall above my head.

"You've saturated your clothing," he growled as he

continued to rub. "It's leaking through yours and into mine."

"Is that a bad thing?"

"Fuck no."

Moaning with excitement, I shoved myself against him, pressing hard and twisting to make sure each of his strokes hit my clit just right. I clung to his shirt, refusing to let go, but he wasn't making any effort to pull away.

Bracing my ass with his palms, his pace picked up, his hips surging against me, pressing his cock hard. He growled and groaned, which only made my pulse surge faster.

The symbols on my wrists blazed bright green, the exact color of his skin.

He snarled and moved faster, his hips flexing as he pushed against my clit.

Whimpering, I wrenched his shirt up, exposing his taut green skin. Nice abs. Nice chest. Wonderful shoulders and arms. I sucked on one nipple, then the other, and they hardened.

My body tightened, my orgasm rising with each crest until I crashed, a tsunami pummeling the shore, driving halfway across a continent.

Shudders consumed my frame, and I clung to him, my moans wrenching out of me over and over.

He groaned and his cock jerked in his pants. Pressing harder, he ground against me.

My body gave way again, flying all the way to the stars.

Our movements slowed, and I pressed my face against his bare chest, my breathing ragged.

"We need to keep stuff like this from happening," he said in a hoarse voice.

"We didn't have penetration."

"I want to fuck you hard until you come."

"Keep saying stuff like that, and I'm going to strip and climb into your bed, dragging you along with me."

"I'm not going to dare you." His chuckle rang out, low and deep. The heady sound made the symbols on my wrists flare again before backing off to a pale green. Tiny yellow flowers had formed near the vines, plus new baby green leaves. I had a feeling this meant something, but I was too focused on my body's hum of satisfaction to bring it up.

I slid my legs down the sides of his thighs and settled my feet on the floor, releasing his shirt to fall back down over his abs. It was a shame to cover them when I still wanted to lick them.

"We're walking on thin ice," he said. "We need to stay away from each other from now on."

What if I didn't want to stay away?

"I still need help with my book," I said.

He groaned and ran his claws through his hair.

"Does that ever slice it?" I asked.

His hand paused. "What?"

"Your hair." I flicked my fingers that way. "Claws. Do you inadvertently cut your hair when you run your claws through it?"

He frowned. "Why would I?"

I shook my head. "Okay, forget about that. Back to the book. We could work on the break-up scene. That shouldn't test us too much."

"Why a breakup? I thought you wrote romance."

"I do, but most romances have a black moment."

His head tilted. "Why?"

Did he realize he was fingering my hair, gliding the pad of his thumb across a few strands, over and over? Far be it for me to point it out. "A black moment is where the couple tests their inner conflict. It gives them a chance to overcome whatever was holding them back."

"What could hold them back?"

Did I dare? Sure, why not? "Well, let's pretend he was hurt by someone in the past." I didn't quite dare to make this about Vrok. "Say . . . his parents abandoned him. He might avoid loving someone so they don't abandon him and cause even greater pain."

"Sounds simple but stupid on his part."

"Well, you know how people are."

A tic formed in his temple. "I suppose I do."

"In the black moment, she might do something that makes him think she's going to abandon him, and as a knee-jerk reaction, he ends things and backs away. Personally, I try to avoid the more clichéd black moments like this one because it's often a matter of poor communication. I prefer to almost kill one of them instead."

His laugh snorted out. "Yeah, death would be a black moment."

"In the abandonment scenario we're talking about, I use a moment like that to give him a chance to realize that if he doesn't try to make things work, he'll lose her. The black moment is near the end of the book and is followed by a happy for now or a happily ever after. That's the rule in romance."

"What if one of them dies?"

"Then it's not romance; that's a tragedy, and I don't betray my readers by writing them."

"I see." He appeared to be thinking.

I was struggling not to stare at the huge wet spot on the front of his pants. How much cum did an orc produce?

Something I needed to look up once I was home.

CHAPTER 9

VROK

"You've got a deal," I told Nyxor on the phone two days later.

Thankfully, Seyla had stayed away, and when I caught her working in her front yard—in shorts and a cropped top—I hadn't stared at her for more than ten minutes.

My hard-on faded when I stepped away from the window.

"When do you have an appointment at Monster Mingle?" I asked my friend.

"Too late, dude," he said. "I went yesterday; Grannie Vi and Uncle Bub have fixed me up with three women. My first date's tonight."

"You want to double?"

"Not yet, but I might hit you up if things don't go well."

"Alright."

"Stop in to see Grannie Vi yourself," he said. "I take it you and Seyla aren't hitting it off?"

I growled.

He laughed. "Or you are. Let me guess, you two gave into the mating bond."

"We didn't have—" I was not using the word penetration with my friend. There was a line, and I wouldn't cross it.

"Why not take her out? See if there's something there?" he asked.

"Because I don't want to date anyone. I'm not trusting my heart to a woman again."

"Then why go to Monster Mingle?"

"I need a distraction."

"I think you need to take things further with Seyla."

"I'm not doing it," I shouted, then lowered my voice. "Sorry. I don't mean to yell at you."

"You're frustrated. I assume it's the bond roaring inside you. I read a bit about it online last night. Those chemicals are wreaking havoc with you, my friend. You might as well smile and give in, especially if she's equally interested."

She was more than interested.

"I'm not going to give in." I was stubborn if nothing else.

He sighed. "If you say so. Hey, I've got to go. Let me know how things go at Monster Mingle."

"I will."

I hung up and dialed the matchmaking service.

"Dream dates are us," Grannie called out in a cheery

voice. "You've reached Monster Mingle. How can we help?"

"This is Vrok Tregartill. I'd like to set up an appointment."

"Do you have time to stop in this afternoon? We had a cancellation. A birdman backed out at the last minute. He met his match in a naga this morning and doesn't want to make his naga mad. I guess a naga's bite can be lethal."

I blinked for a second, processing the idea of a birdman and a naga hooking up. "What time?"

"Three?"

"Alright, three it is." I ended the call and went to my office. Once I sat, however, I couldn't find my focus.

"I'm not betraying Seyla by going to a matchmaker," I said, tossing my pen on top of my papers.

Merith heard my voice and swooped into my office, landing hard on my desk. He skidded across the surface, sweeping papers off, barely catching himself with his fluttering wings. The papers sailed onto the floor. Again.

With a sigh, I picked them up. "You need to practice your landings little guy. You're coming in way too fast."

He squawked and flapped his wings before settling again, his attention locked on me.

Outside, someone started a weed whacker, the whirring whine a complete distraction.

I gave up on my paperwork and leaned back in my chair.

Merith took flight and soared from the room. When he scratched at the back door, I got up to let him out.

"Don't go far," I said. "I have an appointment in . . ." I glanced at my watch, "twenty-five minutes."

He gave me an odd look before flying down to the lawn. Scratching at the soil, he pecked, gobbling up bugs.

I sat on the back steps.

The weed whacker came closer, and I didn't need to look that way to know who ran the device. Seyla was working on her yard again. Didn't she have anything better to do? Good thing we had the fence to keep us apart. Not that I couldn't leap over it if I wanted to—which I did.

Had she changed out of her shorts and t-shirt?

Rising, I went over to my fence and peeked through a thin gap between the wooden slats.

Seyla wore noise-reduction headphones, and she must have music piping in through them, because she sashayed across the back section of her yard, chopping tall grass with her device as she went.

She wore a white sundress with big yellow flowers that made her legs look long and amazing. The skirt swayed with her movements, gliding along the backs of her thighs.

My cock stirred, sensing action, and I didn't have to look at my wrists to know the green vines were flaring.

I backed away from the fence and, turning, half-raced into my house, slamming the door behind me. I locked it for good measure.

Realizing it was time to leave for town, I strode down the front hall, snatching the keys from the table as I passed.

I jogged to my truck sitting in my driveway and climbed inside, starting the engine.

It didn't take long to reach the downtown area, and I parked in a spot not far from the entrance to Monster Mingle.

As I got out of my truck, the front door opened, and something golden zipped out.

A pixie? I supposed they dated too, though they were awfully tiny. I liked my women Seyla-sized. Petite compared to my orc frame, but not so small that we wouldn't fit together. Not that I planned to sleep with anyone Vi fixed me up with.

For whatever reason, that also felt like betrayal.

With a grumble, I opened the front door of Monster Mingle and stepped inside.

"Right on time," Grannie Vi called out from an open doorway partway down a hall behind the empty reception area.

"Come right in, my boy," Uncle Bub chimed in from inside the office. "Settle and we'll fix you up." He cackled. "Get it, Vi? Fix you up. It has a double meaning."

"That it does, Bub. That it does," she said.

I dropped into the chair across from their large desk, taking in the light summer breeze stirring the curtains in the window behind them, plus the fond way they glanced at each other.

Vi wore a bright orange dress, and Bub was dressed in a blue suit with a matching orange bow tie.

"What can we do for you?" Grannie Vi asked.

"I'd like to meet some women, go out on a date or two," I said.

"Lovely." Grannie Vi clapped. She tugged her keyboard closer and frowned at the monitor. "Let's go through your basic criteria, add some details that show who you truly are, and see what my magical device comes up with."

"Magical?" I asked. Last I knew, the treaty between monsters and humans forbids most magic, though simple spells were permitted.

"Tylik helped us out with a lovely spell," she said, beaming. "He cast it on the computer. Just a little love potion number twelve."

"You'll be surprised at how accurate our matches are now," Uncle Bub said. "They're darn near perfect."

"Oh, definitely perfect," Grannie said. Her gaze shot to a shelf mounted on the wall. "Aw, Bub, there's only one bag left, and I suspect Vrok might need one soon." Her elbow nudged Bub. "We need to make up more bags." She wrinkled her nose at me. "Each couple successfully matched receives a goodie bag from us. We'll have one with your name on it once you've proposed, so stop back here then."

"I'm not proposing to anyone." Why was I picturing Seyla dressed in a gorgeous gown, walking down the aisle to stand beside me at the altar? Orcs didn't marry in that way; our relationships were completed once we'd fully bonded. But humans enjoyed the pomp and flowers stuff, and I was sure Seyla would too.

I growled, wishing I could stop thinking about her.

"Vi knows the right toys to give for a honeymoon," Bub said, also winking.

My skin prickled, and the symbols on my wrists sparkled before settling back to a low simmer.

"What do you want to know about me?" I asked.

They ran through general questions that would fit with any dating service before jumping into the specifics of what I was looking for.

"Any body build?" Grannie asked, her fingers poised over the keyboard.

"I like a woman with generous curves," I said, thinking of Seyla.

"A woman, then. Men if they fit?" Bub asked.

"I guess I'm hetero."

"Alright." Vi squinted at the computer screen. "You're tall for an orc. Does her height matter?"

"Petite would be nice. The top of her head could come to about here." I made a chopping motion at my nipple line. My mind shot to when I ground against Seyla, and she'd sucked on them. That simple touch made my cum shoot from me, blasting the front of my pants.

I needed to stop thinking about burying my cum someplace else.

"We realize physical description is not the only thing you're seeking in a female," Bub said. "Any particular personality traits you'd like to be matched with?"

"A good sense of humor." I frowned, thinking. "It would be nice if she enjoyed romance."

"Reading or living it?" Grannie Vi asked.

"Why not both?"

"Exactly," she said with a denture-filled grin.

"Do you do much physical activity?" Bub asked, staring at the screen.

I kept picturing all the activities I'd like to do with Seyla. In my bed. On the back deck, beneath the stars. The grass would feel nice on my backside while she rode me.

My huff rang out. Why couldn't I stop thinking about her?

"I like to remain active," I said.

"Oh!" Grannie Vi's word was punctuated with a ping from the computer. "That was fast. We have a match. We have a match!"

The printer sitting on the side of the desk started whirring, and a piece of paper slid out.

"Here she is," Bub said, standing and taking the paper. "You're lucky lady." He handed it to me.

Seyla Felicia Anderson.

I jerked the paper back at them, and it slid across the desk and kept going, smacking into the wall beside Uncle Bub. "Someone different, please."

Seyla had been to Monster Mingle? When had she come in to find a match, and how many dates had she been on already?

"The computer has a spell case on it," Grannie Vi said, sternly shaking her wrinkled finger my way. "It will only match you with the mate of your dreams."

"I don't dream about Seyla." Not too much.

"I suppose we could exclude her from the results,"

Bub said sourly. "I can't believe you're refusin' a magically crafted match."

"She's my next-door neighbor," I said, as if that was enough reason not to date her.

"You could combine your properties," Grannie said.

"Could you find me someone else?" I asked. "Please?"

Anyone but the woman I couldn't stop thinking about.

"Very well," Bub said with a sigh. He leaned around Grannie Vi and tapped on the keyboard. "She won't be part of this search."

Another ping rang out, and the printer ejected a second piece of paper.

Grannie reached around Bub to tug it off the printer, handing it to me.

Seyla Felicia Anderson.

With a snarl, I rose and fled from their office.

CHAPTER 10
SEYLA

As I was finishing up my weed whacking and putting my equipment away in my tiny shed, Merith landed on my shoulder. He ruffled his wings, sat, and started purring.

"Oh, hey, little one," I said, stroking his gorgeous wings.

He leaned his head against my hand, his purr getting louder.

"While it's nice to see you, does Vrok know you're visiting me?" My neighbor tended to keep a close eye on his dragonette friend. He was a wonderful pet parent. "Maybe I should bring you back to him."

I stepped inside my house to get a drink of water first.

Sriracha barreled down the hall and meowed at Merith, who flew down to greet my kitty friend.

When the hum of a big engine rang out from the

street, I walked to my front door and peered through the tall window on the side of the door.

Vrok parked his truck, got out, and entered his house.

Merith flew up and landed on my shoulder, looking out the window as avidly as me.

Sriracha followed, sauntering down the hall. He only made it halfway before flopping on the floor. He rolled onto his back, begging for belly rubs.

Merith purred and rubbed his head against my cheek.

"You must've escaped, you sneaky dragonette," I cooed to the preening creature. "I need to bring you home before he gets worried."

Because we'd discussed working on my book again, I grabbed my phone.

Vrok had locked the gate on his side, but he'd only used a hook and eye. A thin stick slid up from beneath took care of that little problem.

I strode up his back steps, crossed his deck, and knocked on his door.

He scowled through the glass panel, but his eyes widened when he took in Merith riding on my shoulder.

"Are you luring my dragonette?" he asked after he'd opened the door.

With a heavy sigh, I brushed past him, striding down the hall to his small kitchen. The floor layout was the same as mine, as was the exterior of our houses; two of a long row of them on this street.

Merith leapt off my shoulder and flew back down the hall.

"I'm not a pixie or sprite," I pointed out. "I can't lure anyone into doing anything they don't want to."

His scowl deepened.

I held up my hand. "And, no, I didn't cast a spell on you." Reaching forward, I poked one of the symbols on his wrist. "You're the one who roped us into this orc marriage."

"We're not married."

"Nice of you to point that out." I wasn't sure why my mood toward him had turned sour. Maybe because he'd irked me when he told me I had to stay away from him, like I was the only one part of our mutually satisfying humping session against the wall.

It was hard to maintain an upbeat attitude with a guy who grumbled and pushed me away all the time.

"I'm sorry." His shoulders softened. "I realize you didn't ask for this any more than I did. We're in it together, I suppose."

"Merith landed on my shoulder as I was putting my weed whacker away. I brought him back."

"Big mistake on my part," he said. "Distracted, I went into town, totally forgetting I'd let him outside. Thanks for watching out for him."

"I don't mind. He's a sweet dragonette."

"My parents raise them, and they're rare. A mating pair may only have two or three eggs during their life-time, and it's common for only one or two to live to maturity."

"Merith is special."

He gave me a slight smile. "Would you like to come

into the living room? We can talk. Someone I know brought me some amazing cookies, and I don't want to eat them all by myself." He patted his washboard abs.

Funny how he only had to be slightly nice to me, and I preened like Merith, eager for pats.

I liked Vrok. I'd be foolish to turn down his offer.

"Get the cookies, and I'll bring glasses of water," I said.

He took the cookie container from the counter while I filled glasses at the sink, and I followed him down the hall to the living room, where we settled on the sofa.

"Are you sure you dare to sit this close to me?" I had to ask.

"I can handle it." His heated gaze met mine, making flutters erupt in my belly.

"I brought my phone." I held it up. "We could go through another part of my book if you have time."

"Not a steamy part."

A lot of my book was steamy, but I wasn't going to point that out. "Heat is all about perspective." That was neutral enough.

At his cautious nod, I scrolled through my book to the section I felt needed a bit of work. "So, in this part, the storm is fully upon them."

"I assume they're trapped together."

"Inside his snug log cabin. The power has gone out, and he's lighting a fire in the woodstove. They just returned from bringing in wood, and they're both soaked to the bone from the rain."

He grinned. "That's clever on your part."

"What do you mean?"

"I assume they have to take off their wet clothing."

"Yeah, that's the point, I suppose. It's almost guaranteed heat, but this scene is about more than that. They're growing closer together, and it's a chance for him to show caring, not just sexual desire."

"*Very* wise."

I tilted my head, watching as he ate a cookie in two bites. "Do you read much romance?"

"Some. I like the steamy bits as much as anyone else," he said, his smile widening.

"Many readers adore them. They're not gratuitous. They help enhance the romance. As an author, I use them to show commitment between the couple. Some authors show the couple having sex early in the book, and that has its place too. You know, a desire that's explosive enough they can't keep their hands off each other from the moment they meet." I coughed, hoping he didn't think I was referring to us.

Although, we did have an explosive romance, and we *had* rushed into intimacy fast, though that could be the orc bond speaking.

"Maybe we wouldn't want each other without the symbols," I said.

"Maybe." He waved a cookie at my phone. "Read the scene, and I'll let you know if I think it needs changes."

I cleared my throat and stared at my screen. "She's breathing fast from carrying loads of wood into the house, and it kind of breaks him."

"Why?"

"Because he doesn't like seeing her work hard. He wants to take care of her."

"I understand that."

I shot him a grin. "Did you feel like taking over my weed whacking when you were peeking through the fence earlier?"

"You noticed."

"Just vaguely." Actually, I was hyperaware of Vrok all the time. I swore I could almost hear him breathing when I lay in my bed at night despite him lying a complete building away.

"Your yard looks fantastic. I need to work more on mine."

"I love having my own house. I've lived in apartments until now. But my books are doing well, and I've saved a lot of my income."

"It's amazing that you can make a living as a writer."

"It's not common. I've been incredibly lucky." I stiffened my spine. "Actually, it's not just about luck. I work hard, and it's paying off."

"You seem to enjoy it."

"I love it. Who wouldn't want to make up stories all day long?" But enough about me. I held up my phone and read from my book. "This is from her point of view."

"You shouldn't have carried any of the wood." I read. *Lifting me, he took me over to the sofa, though he placed me on my feet beside it. He stripped off my shirt and pants, using the tender touch of a doting parent.*

"Parent?" Vrok asked.

"It shows caring, and that this isn't sexual."

"Believe me, if he's removing her clothing, it's sexual."

"I'm sure to some extent it is, but in this part of the scene, it's not about sex."

He huffed.

"Are you looking at me sexually?" I asked, determined to prove to him that guys didn't always see women in that light, not if they were doing something unrelated to sex.

"I try not to," he said with a wince.

"Oh, shit, please don't tell me you're getting a hard-on right now."

"I'm not sure I can tell you that."

"Jeez, Vrok. I'm reading from my book. This is a serious scene." I might sound firm, but inside, I was snickering. He was too cute. And I didn't mind that he was turned on just by being with me.

I was falling for him when it would be the biggest mistake of my life. Was this the bond speaking? Maybe a bit, but I'd liked him before the symbols appeared on my wrists. And they weren't there when he pumped his fingers inside me while I lay splayed wide for him on the counter.

Something I'd like to do right now.

"Don't get that look in your eyes, Seyla," he said in warning, leaning away from me.

"What look is that?"

"The one that says I make your body throb with my touch."

"I'm not sure I can tell you it doesn't," I said, tossing his own words back at him.

"Seyla." He stroked the hair off my face and took my phone, laying it on the table in front of the sofa. Leaning forward, he kissed me softly, gently, so tenderly it made my heart twist into a knot.

When he lifted his head, his gaze remained locked on mine. He glided his knuckles down my neck, making my skin tingle.

"What am I going to do with you?" he asked.

Love me, I wanted to say, but that would be pushing.

"I should leave," I said, though I made no move to slide off the sofa as his knuckles continued moving downward, stroking between the crests of my breasts revealed by my sundress and across one of the mounds. The nipple tightened, and fire shot from my breast to my groin.

My moan slipped out. "Tell me to leave." If he did, I'd try to obey.

"Just one second longer." He nudged my sundress down, revealing my breast. Since I was working outside and alone, I'd gone braless. "This ripe bud needs some attention, don't you think?"

Despite him making the accusation, he was the one who was lulling me with his smooth-as-whiskey voice and the rough stroke of his knuckles.

"One taste," he said, bending forward to suck my nipple into his mouth.

When he ran his tongue across it, I groaned. I arched my spine, pushing my breast toward him.

He slid his hand down my side and cupped one side of my ass, squeezing.

I collapsed backward onto the sofa, and he followed, tugging and licking my nipple.

I splayed my legs wide. How could I do anything else?

He massaged my thighs with smooth circles, slowly approaching the juncture where I craved his touch.

A quick slice of his claws severed my underwear. I should protest, tell him he needed to stop cutting my clothing, but all I could think of was how much I ached for the drive of his fingers inside me.

No, I wanted his cock driving inside me. Were we ready to take that final step?

I might be, but it was clear he was not. I wanted forever with Vrok, and I wouldn't spoil it by giving into a single moment.

He stroked through my wetness, groaning against my breast. Leaving my nipple, he exposed the other, giving it equal attention. All the while, his fingers teased, gliding down my slit but never sliding within me, never touching my clit.

I writhed beneath him, a moaning wreck already.

When he pushed what felt like three fingers inside me, I whimpered with excitement.

He pumped, keeping a steady pace, driving me to a fever.

His thumb found my clit, stroking it.

My body made sucking sounds—so did his mouth on my breast. I relished the heat of it, how much my body was into this moment.

Lifting his head, he continued to suck on my nipple while watching my face. His fingers pushed deeper, and he grinned when I moaned.

My body kept rising toward the peak before slipping back downward.

His fingers went faster, and each time he tugged them out, he twisted them to hit my G-spot.

He pressed down hard on my clit, dragging his claw across it.

I shot through the roof. Through the clouds.

Hell, I soared past the space station.

CHAPTER II
VROK

I had a feeling I wasn't going to be able to resist Seyla. But my mind told me I had to take care, or I'd get hurt again. I needed to push her away.

We sat on the sofa after I'd loved her body; me trying to keep from lifting my hand and licking her essence off my fingers, her staring at the plate of cookies, still breathing fast.

Color made her cheeks extra pretty. I liked that I could mess her up, make her flush, and give her so much pleasure.

I liked it too much.

"At this rate, I'm not going to have any underwear left," she said with a snort.

I shouldn't take pride in shredding them, but I did.

"We should go to Mystic Mixtures," I said.

"Tylik's magical apothecary? It's funny, I heard it's on Main Street, but when I look for it, I can't find it."

"It's shielded from humans, though a few have found

their way inside. Those with precognition or a sixth sense, I suppose." I swallowed, sensing what I had to say wouldn't be well received. "We can ask him for a spell to break this bond."

She turned a wide-eyed gaze my way. "Is that what you want?"

It was what I needed. "What I want can't come into this."

"Why not?" Her head tilted as she watched me. "Does whatever's between us have to be complex?"

"I don't want to be with anyone." Standing, I started pacing across my living room.

"Alright, then," she said tightly, standing. "I don't want a forced relationship any more than you."

"You don't?" Pausing, I scratched my head. "I thought you wanted to be with me."

Rising from the sofa, her chin lifted. "Maybe I don't any longer."

CHAPTER 12

SEYLA

It was a lie.

I'd wanted to be with him almost from the moment I met him. It was ironic, really. Guys regularly threw themselves at me, and I wasn't picky. If I liked someone, I went out with them.

But I'd saved my heart for one special guy.

I thought that could be Vrok, but he seemed to be hell-bent on proving we didn't belong together. I wouldn't fight him. If he didn't want to be with me, I would make myself stop caring.

It hurt, but what else could I do?

"Do you have time now to go into town to get the ingredients for a spell to end this?" I asked.

He blinked at me, his mouth sliding ajar.

"What? Do you think I'm going to continue throwing myself at you while you keep doing things like what just happened?" I swept my hand toward the sofa. "Then listen to you tell me you don't want to be with me? I like you, Vrok, but I don't need you."

He continued staring, obviously stunned by my words. Finally, he shook his head. "Yes, I can go into town. Right now if you have time."

I looked down at my clothing. "I do need to put on new underwear."

"I can wait."

"Maybe things will be easier between us if we both acknowledge we don't want to be together," I offered as he held open the front door for me to step outside. We'd take his truck, of course. He wouldn't fit inside my small compact.

"Maybe." He watched me. What did he see? Hopefully a woman who was going to scrub Vrok Tregartill out of her soul.

Merith swooped through the opening and landed on my shoulder. He scooted close to my neck and ran the side of his head across my hair, making it swirl around me from static.

At least *he* liked me.

"I'll be right back." I hustled over to my house, Merith riding along with me. It didn't take long to put on a bra, new panties, and a dress that wouldn't remind me that Vrok had just tugged it down to reach my breasts.

When I returned outside, Vrok took Merith from me and placed him inside his house. Since his truck was locked, I waited.

Returning, Vrok opened the passenger door and lifted me inside.

"I can climb in myself," I said.

"I want to help."

"Why?" I studied his face.

He appeared as bewildered by the gesture as me. "I wanted to. It's alright, isn't it?"

I shrugged, my mood lightening, though I wasn't sure why. "Sure. No problem."

He nodded slowly as he shut the door and went around to the driver's side. Once he'd climbed in, he leaned across me and secured the buckle.

"I could've done that too," I said.

"I don't understand what's happening." He blinked at me slowly, frowning.

"Is it the bond?" That must be it. He wouldn't do it because he wanted to; no, because he *had* to.

I would hate to be in a position where some kind of genetic thing controlled my actions. My heart might be pulling me toward Vrok, but at least it wasn't a chemical reaction I couldn't resist.

It almost made me feel sad for Vrok.

And us.

"We'll break this," I said, my resolve thickening inside me. "Then you won't feel compelled to do things like that any longer."

"You're right." He swallowed. "You're gorgeous, you know."

What good did a statement like that do in this situation? "Thanks."

"If I wanted to have a relationship, if I wasn't still hurt from Margie, I'd be all over you."

"You already are." I felt the need to point that out. "Oh but wait. That's not you. That's the bond."

He stared down at the markings on his wrists for a long moment before buckling up. "You're right. It's the bond."

"The sooner we break it, the quicker we can go back to being friends. Maybe I won't want you anymore once it's over."

He cocked his head my way. "You won't? Is that how it works with humans?"

I held up my arms, flexing the matching symbols on my wrists. "Maybe these are driving me as much as they are you. Once they're gone, I might not think you're cute or sweet any longer. I might not want to suck your cock or ride you until you fill me with cum."

He growled, shifting in his seat. "Maybe don't mention things like that."

"Sorry." My snort slipped out. "Actually, it would make things much simpler if I didn't feel that way. I'd love to be able to shut off my emotions that easily."

"You're right," he said, backing down his driveway. "I'd like to shut them off myself."

And that was the problem here. Would removing the bond make me stop longing to be with him?

It looked like we might soon find out.

Vrok parked his truck in town and leaned across me, undoing the buckle.

"Um, try to restrain yourself?" I said, my hands lifted. I chuckled. My heart should be breaking. Instead, I found this funny.

"Yes, sorry," he said with a frown. He scooted out of the vehicle while I opened my door. When his hands reached out to lift me from the truck, he snapped them back. "This is so strange."

I stepped onto the sidewalk with him.

We walked down Main Street, and I still didn't see a sign for a magical apothecary.

Vrok stopped in front of a brick building and opened a door that didn't appear to be there until he touched it.

"That was a wall," I said as I stepped inside. "There was no door."

"You're right," he said, following me into the apothecary.

Huh.

Pausing, I closed my eyes and sucked in the spicy-herbal scent common in health food stores. But the smell wasn't the only thing worth checking out. I scooted ahead of Vrok down a long aisle where shelves on each side were full of bottles and oddly shaped clear containers full of colorful stuff. Some looked like the herbs I was familiar with, but others held things that glowed with a low, magical light. Other items lay in bins, from long, black, stick-like things to open plastic containers holding round, gleaming yellow balls.

When I reached out, Vrok grabbed my hand and tugged my arm back.

"It's better not to touch anything here," he said.

"Oh, right," I said in awe. "It's amazing."

"That it is. It's a place few humans will ever see."

"I understand why."

With his big palm resting on my back, he urged me to the back of the big room and over to a counter.

Tylik bustled behind it wearing a white tunic much like I'd see on a pharmacist. His golden hair and pointed elf ears, in addition to his height and almost magically gorgeous appearance, proved he was not human, however.

Hearing us, he turned, his gaze sliding from me to Vrok and back again.

"Seyla. Welcome." He approached the counter. "You, too, Vrok. What can I do for you today?"

"We need a spell," Vrok said, holding up his arms to show off the symbols.

I did the same so he could see that they matched.

"Ah, yes." Tylik frowned. "You two are bonded. Does Kate know, Seyla? She'll be happy to hear—"

"That's just it," I said. "We want to end the bond." Actually, I didn't, but I was going to ride this out with Vrok.

"Why?"

"Because," I jerked my shoulder Vrok's way, "he's nursing a broken heart from someone named Margie, and he seems to have decided he doesn't want to be with anyone else."

Vrok had the grace to squirm, though he recovered quickly. "We don't want to be forced into anything."

"In that, he's right," I said. Sadly, I wasn't sure I felt forced. But if Vrok did, I didn't want him.

If he held out his hand solely due to interest alone, without a bond driving him, I'd be happy to take it.

"Bonds like this are an orc thing," Tylik said.

"You don't have a spell that will end it?" Vrok asked, his hand still resting on my spine.

It felt good there.

I bit off the thought the moment it occurred to me.

"I didn't exactly say that," Tylik said. "Are you capable of conducting a spell? Few are."

"I've never cast one, but how tough can it be?" Vrok asked.

"Harder than you'd believe." Tylik frowned, thinking. "There's someone in town who might be able to perform the spell for you, however. I can put the ingredients together, give you the recipe, so to speak, and you can ask him if he's willing to do it."

"Who can perform the spell?" I asked.

"Raze."

"An ogre?" I said.

"If he'd chosen to remain with his people, he'd be King Raze to everyone around him. His lineage has the ability to perform spells such as this."

A wedding planner performing a spell? But what else could I expect in a town renamed Monsterville?

Tylik gathered a variety of ingredients and placed most in containers. The rest, he left loose in a paper bag, handing it to Vrok. "Are you sure you want to do this?"

"Why wouldn't we?" I asked.

"Because it's a bond, something to treasure and hold tight, not toss aside. Few ever meet their fated mates."

"It's not what Vrok wants," I said.

Tylik's gaze met mine, and I found sorrow there. He could see I was in pain. "I'm sorry."

My heart deadened. "Thanks."

As Vrok and I left the apothecary and returned to his truck, my pulse took a nosedive. I wasn't sure I wanted to end our bonding, not if it was going to hurt this much. But then I reminded myself this was forced on both of us. Maybe once the spell was broken, I wouldn't like Vrok.

Although, I had a feeling it was going to take more than removing symbols from my wrists to make that happen.

CHAPTER 13

VROK

I should be grateful Seyla was being so good about this.

Why, then, did my chest hurt so much?

"It's the bond," I said as I lifted Seyla into my truck. As soon as I realized I was leaning in to buckle her, I backed away, my hands lifting. "I'm sorry."

"Hey, no problem. I'm short. Your truck is tall. There's no harm in you helping me."

With a nod, I went around and climbed into the driver's seat, starting the vehicle and backing it out of the spot.

"Since it's all caused by the bond," she said, "I welcome ending it."

My breath caught. "You do?"

"Of course. Don't you?"

"I do." I made sure my voice sounded confident in this. Inside, I wasn't. But I couldn't back out of it now. She didn't want me any more than I did her. It was fake.

Once the bond was broken, we'd probably laugh about it and shake our heads, unable to believe we'd almost fallen for it.

"Once it's over," she said, staring out the side window as I drove toward Elisa and Raze's wedding planning business. "I won't have this overwhelming urge to glide my fingers up and down your cock or beg you to take me doggie style."

My cock surged to attention. "Just doggie style?"

She shot me a smile. "Or over the back of the couch. Missionary style's boring, don't you think?"

"Maybe it was only boring because of who you were doing it with."

"Perhaps." She bit down on her lower lip before releasing it. "There are other positions, of course. I could ride you."

"You totally could." I shouldn't be gushing about this.

"Or you could take me against a wall," she added.

"We shouldn't be talking about this." I shifted in my seat, trying to find a comfortable position with a stiff rod slamming around inside my pants.

"You're right." She shifted herself, and it didn't take any imagination on my part to picture her glistening passage or her swollen clit. "We could hold a party once this is finished. We could invite a bunch of single people and make the rounds, looking for new people to be with."

"Is that what you want to do?" I asked.

"Don't you?"

"I guess." I couldn't imagine dating.

Funny how I'd barely thought about Margie for days, and when I did think of her, the pinch in my chest was gone. All I could think of during the day was Seyla, and at night, I dreamed about being with her.

The bond, I reminded myself. It wasn't me or her or us.

I parked in front of Elisa and Raze's wedding planning business, and we got out of the vehicle—me barely resisting carrying Seyla into the building.

"Hey," Elisa called out when we stepped inside. Her gaze locked on our wrists, and a big smile appeared on her pretty face. "Hey, hey, hey! You two!" Dancing over to us, she took one of each of our hands and swayed back and forth. "You two are mated? Congratulations. Hey, Raze, guess who's here to plan a wedding!"

"Oh, no, we're not," Seyla said, but Elisa didn't seem to hear.

She danced down the hall, calling out over her shoulder. "Come on back, you two. I realize you'll probably get other quotes, but know right now, me and Raze would be delighted to help you set up the perfect day."

CHAPTER 14

SEYLA

I rolled my eyes at Vrok.

He chuckled. "If we were planning a wedding, I wouldn't get quotes. I'd definitely go with Elisa and Raze."

"Oh, me too," I said.

We followed her down the hall and into their shared office.

"We're not getting married," I said before we took the seats across from them.

"You're not?" Elisa's gaze fell on our wrists again. "I don't understand."

"We're unwillingly bonded," I said firmly.

Vrok frowned my way. Why the look? He was the one who'd finally convinced me we needed to end this.

"We came here because Tylik gave us the ingredients for a spell that can break the bond," Vrok said. "He indicted you might be able to perform it for us, Raze."

"Oh, I see." Raze grunted. Leaning back in his chair,

he steepled his hands on his chest. "I do know a few spells that might help you, but I don't believe any of them are exactly what is needed to break an orc fated mate bonding."

Vrok set the paper bag on their shared desk. "Tylik included the recipe, so to speak, for the spell."

"Let me take a look." Raze dragged the bag across the desk and opened it, peering inside. "Hmm." His gaze met ours. "There is one spell . . ." His frown deepened. "Are you sure you don't want to hold onto the bond? It's rare for anyone to find their fated mate." He lifted Elisa's hand and kissed her knuckles.

She sent him a soft, loving smile that made my heart twist into a knot.

There was a time when I'd hoped Vrok would look at me the same way. Now, I wasn't sure I'd believe it if he did. Love should never be forced.

"We want to break it," I said again.

Vrok shot me another odd look. "We do."

Why did he sound hesitant now? Ah, yes, the bond. It was speaking for him.

"If you two are completely sure," Raze said. "I'll perform the spell tomorrow evening. Spells work better at night, and there's a full moon tomorrow. That'll help."

"We're sure," I said, ignoring my gut telling me I shouldn't speak up.

"Go home. Give this one night," Raze said. "And call me in the morning if you still want to break the bond."

Vrok stood. "Thank you." He held out his hand to me to help me rise before snatching it back.

"I recommend you spend tonight together," Raze called out as we crossed the front room, heading for the door.

"We don't want to," I shouted back.

Raze appeared in the open doorway. "It's my condition to perform this."

"I'm not giving her penetration," Vrok snarled.

I nodded, giving him an approving grin.

"You two are out of your minds," Raze said softly, coming toward us. He lifted his voice. "I don't suggest you have sex, though I'm not sure it'll make much difference."

I wasn't sure what that meant.

"But before you do something this drastic, I want you both to think long and hard about what you're throwing away. A fated mate bond is to be cherished, treasured. It's never torn asunder unless the two are completely sure that's what they want."

"Have any couples done it before?" I asked as Vrok opened the front door.

"Only one," Raze said.

Elisa peeked around him at us, her gaze full of concern.

"What happened?" Vrok asked.

"It ended," Raze said. "But they hated each other after that."

CHAPTER 15
VROK

I lifted Seyla into my truck. She sighed and shot me a look I couldn't define.

Once I was seated and ensured she was buckled, I just sat there, staring forward.

"I don't want to hate you," I said.

"I feel the same." Her second sigh bled out. "Do you think, once the bond is broken, we won't feel *anything* for each other?"

"That's my assumption." Funny how I welcomed but didn't welcome falling out of love with Seyla.

I couldn't love her. If I felt the emotion, it was created by the bond. But it still hurt to think of ending things with her, as if my chest would be empty when she was no longer there to fill it up.

"What should we do tonight?" I asked. This could be the last time we were together. We might build memories that would feel bittersweet, or we'd look back on them and shake our heads, wondering what we'd been thinking.

She turned in her seat to face me. "No idea."

"There's a carnival set up on the edge of town. Would you like to go?"

Her smile filled the hole that had started to gape wide open in my chest. "Sounds fun."

"Now or later?" I asked. "It's . . ." A glance at the center console showed four-thirty. "We could get some dinner first if you'd like."

"I don't mind eating whatever we find at the carnival."

"I should get Merith," I said.

"I can check on Sriracha and meet you back at your truck."

I drove through town and parked in my driveway.

It wasn't long before we were back inside my truck, traveling toward the carnival. I parked in the grassy lot along with numerous others, staring toward the improvised amusement park constructed beyond a mesh fence. Rides shaped like octopi snapped into the sky, and a very tall, mechanical yeti hoisted long tubes full of people and monsters overhead. Fur draped down his sides, and his head kept spinning completely around, his grin shooting in all directions.

As we were crossing the lot to queue up for entrance tickets, we ran into Max and Chastity. Max wore a baby pouch and Sydnee rode strapped to his belly, facing outward. She kicked her legs and grinned at everyone, her attention snapping from one thing to another until

Merith lifted off my shoulder and swooped over to hover in front of her, his wings flapping.

She giggled and reached her fingers toward him while Max and Chastity watched her with complete adoration.

"There you are," someone said from behind us.

Darrow and his wife, Paige, strode over to stand with us.

"She's so beautiful," Paige said, joining Sydnee's fan club. She stooped forward to coo at Max and Chastity's daughter before her hand subtly stroked her abdomen. Were she and Darrow expecting a child?

"We're going to the kiddie section first," Chastity said. "They've got sand tables and face painting." She grinned up at Max. "Sydnee's going to have so much fun."

"You, too, love," he said, leaning over to give her a kiss.

Darrow looked our way. "Want to join us for face painting?"

I glanced at Seyla, but her gaze was focused on a troll-themed rollercoaster weaving around the outer aspect of the park.

"I think we have a troller coaster on our agenda," I said. "But thanks."

Max's gaze went from my wrists to Seyla's, but he didn't comment. I'd fill him in later. Or not. We were going to end it, and after that, the symbols would no longer be there.

With Merith back on my shoulder, we left them and

bought tickets, entering the park.

Seyla's gaze locked on a game where they gave out small stuffed bears for prizes so I guided her in that direction instead.

"I thought we were riding the troller coaster?" she asked with a grin as I nudged her toward the game.

"Eventually." I pointed. "Do you think I've got what it takes to win something for you?"

"I bet you do." She narrowed her gaze at one of the bears with a big yellow bow.

The longing I spied there was enough for me. I'd play the game all night if that's what it took to win it for her.

After paying tokens, I waited in line, watching as other monsters competed. They'd roped off two sections, one for bigger guys like me, the other for humans and smaller monsters. The latter appeared a bit less challenging, but they would want people to feel the competition was fair.

"I believe you need to hit the fake popping creatures with the hammer before they shoot back into the ground," Seyla said. Her grin rose. "It looks like a giant whack-a-mole."

"Why would someone hit a mole?" I asked, thinking of the tiny creatures living below the ground.

"In whack-a-mole, they're no more real than the beasties you'll be trying to hit here." Her gaze fell on the smaller course. "Do you mind if I do that one after you've finished?"

"I'd love to cheer you on."

Her smile widened, and she leaned into my side. "Even if this is fake, I'm having fun."

I was too.

CHAPTER 16

SEYLA

I stood back while Vrok competed.

First, he shucked his t-shirt. Talk about drool-worthy. I wasn't the only one who couldn't take their eyes off the play of muscles across his gorgeous torso. His dark green skin gleamed in the setting sunlight, and he was truly a thing of beauty.

When it was his turn, he stepped up to the troll running the game and they joked a few seconds before the stubby guy with shockingly pink hair and wearing a teal-colored suit handed Vrok an enormous hammer.

I doubted I'd be able to lift it, but Vrok hefted it easily, swinging it loosely through the air with one hand as if testing how it might perform during the game.

Merith leapt off his shoulder, onto mine, and I stroked the tiny pet.

The troll waved to the whack-a-whatever course. I wasn't exactly sure what the creatures were supposed to represent. A gremlin-like thing? They universally wore scowls, though that smoothed to a happy face and a bubbling cackle if the competitor missed.

Vrok nodded to the troll, who hit a button mounted on a pole beside him.

The first gremlin popped up from the ground.

Vrok swung, hitting the fake creature smack in the head. The gremlin shrieked and shot back into the ground. Another popped up about five feet behind the first, and Vrok leapt, soaring across the grassy playing field. He landed solidly and swung, impaling the second gremlin.

They started shooting up faster, and Vrok turned into a blur of motion. He did an intricate dance, leaping from one place to another, never missing a shot when the gremlins leapt from the ground.

I gaped, unable to take my eyes off my not-mate. If the game didn't involve smacking a sledgehammer onto shrieking fake creatures, I'd call what he was doing a poetic dance.

I was a writer, but I couldn't come up with the words to describe how amazing it was to watch him play. It was worth a try.

"His skill is unmatched as he brings the sledge-hammer down," I whispered.

A woman about my age, wearing a bright blue sundress stood nearby. She frowned in my direction, but she didn't say anything. She appeared alone, and while she maintained a neutral expression, I sensed loneliness in her posture. She kept scanning the crowd as if she was worried someone would threaten her.

"He sends fake enemies flying back into the ground," I said, wishing I had a pen and a paper to write this down. "His body moves with grace and finesse."

The woman's eyebrows lifted, and she moved a step closer to me, her silver sandals sinking into the ankle-high grass.

"Each of his swings shows strength, beauty, and awe of the best," I said, having fun crafting my little poem. I usually stuck to books, but sometimes, when the whim struck, I'd write short poems. I didn't share those often.

Would Vrok like this one?

He continued across the course, grunting as he hit one creature after another, rarely missing.

A crowd had gathered, everyone cheering him on, leading me to believe we were all witnessing something rarely seen before. Did most competitors miss? Everyone who'd gone before Vrok hadn't struck true more than half the time.

"His strength and agility are put on display," I said softly.

The woman shot me a smile. "As he brings the hammer to its highest sway."

Cool. Leave it to me to make a new writerly friend at a country fair.

"The fierce warrior with a will of steel shows his prowess as he fights with zeal," I said.

The woman sidled nearer, making no effort to hide her smile. "His muscles ripple with each hit and thrust, filling every onlooker with . . ." her grin widened. "Lust?"

Hell, yeah, lust.

"I'm Brooke, by the way," she said. The sun hit her curly blonde hair bouncing around her shoulders, turning it to gold. If the sun hadn't been quite so bright, I might've missed the shadow around her left eye, well covered with make-up. Had someone hurt her? "I just moved to Monsterville about a month ago."

"I'm Seyla," I said, warming to her quickly. I wanted to give her a hug and tell her everything would be okay, but how could I do that? She'd covered the bruise even if it was still exposed on her soul. I doubted she'd want me to bring attention to it. "I also just moved here, though I've been here long enough to buy a house."

"You're seeing the orc?" she asked.

"Vrok and I are neighbors."

"From your words, I'd say he's more than just a simple neighbor to you. I take it he's yours."

We watched as Vrok finished the course. He'd barely broken a sweat, and he didn't appear to be slowing. When the creatures stopped popping from the ground, he dropped the head of the hammer beside his foot and looked around, grinning.

His gaze landed on me, and he winked.

"Yes, he's mine," I said, my voice filled with pride.

But was he?

After tomorrow, he would be up for grabs to anyone who might want him, even Brooke.

I'd go in the opposite direction.

My heart tightened at the thought.

I wasn't looking forward to telling him goodbye.

CHAPTER 17

VROK

"We have a winner," the troll called out. He bustled over to me on his cloven feet. "Please pick whatever prize you want." He took the hammer from my tight grip and tugged me over to where he had prizes clipped to a tall wooden board.

I held my hand out to Seyla, and when she joined us, I tucked her against my side. The entire time I competed, all I could think of was winning Seyla whatever she wanted.

"Welcome," the troll said, giving Seyla a short bow. He looked at me. "Did you win for your mate?"

In my heart, she was my mate—still—so I nodded.

"Very well," the troll said. "Tell me, lovely human, would you like the huge stuffed rabbit? Or would you prefer a rubber chicken?"

"Really?" Seyla asked, gazing up at me with eyes full of wonder. "You won. What do *you* want?"

"This prize is yours," I said.

"You're giving me stiff competition, then, since I'll compete next, and I assume you get to pick a prize if I win. Don't hold your breath, however. The game looks tough."

"The choice is yours," I said, waving to the stuffed and rubber creatures on display. "What would you like?"

"Oh, that one," she said, pointing to the small bear with the big yellow bow I'd seen her admire earlier. "It's so cute."

"It is yours, my lady," the troll said, removing it from a clip and handing it to her.

"Would you hold him while I play the game?" Seyla said. "Merith, sweetie, go to Vrok."

After I put on my shirt, the dragonette leapt from her to my shoulder, where he started to purr.

I grinned and took the bear from Seyla, noting how soft it was. Almost as soft as Seyla's skin.

"Who's next?" the troll called out.

Seyla lifted her hand. "Me!" She leaned against me, lowering her voice. "I'm not taking my shirt off, however."

What a delight it would be to see her compete like that.

I needed to rip that idea from my mind. This was a sort of date, a chance for us to make sure we truly wanted to end the bond. Her performing without a shirt would make it hard for me to tell her goodnight when the day was over.

The troll handed her a smaller hammer, and I noted

the holes where the creatures would pop out were smaller on the human course as well.

"Allow your gaze to blur a bit," I said, "rather than focus on any particular hole. You're more apt to see the creature rising, and you'll find you act almost seamlessly."

"Says the orc who aced the last competition." She took the hammer and shot me a grin. "I'm aiming for half if I'm lucky."

"You might be surprised."

Sucking in a deep breath, she released it and stepped onto the playing field. When she gave the troll a nod, the game began.

Since I'd already competed, I knew what to expect. What I didn't expect was how enthralled I'd be watching Seyla compete. She darted here and there, slamming down with the hammer. And while she didn't hit them all, she did much better than the half she'd guessed.

When the game finished, she pushed hair off her face and sent me a smile so full of joy, it made my heart seize.

She'd had fun, and that was what truly mattered.

"You've won a prize," the troll cried out, pointing to the lower half of the board.

"You get to pick," Seyla said, taking her bear back when she joined me.

"You don't want two stuffed toys?" I said.

"One for you. One for me."

"Alright, I'll take that one." I pointed to a bear with a pink ribbon, and the troll handed it to me.

"It's cute," Seyla said, bumping them together like she was making a toast. "They're friends."

"Definitely friends, like us."

She looked up at me, searching my face, though I wasn't sure what she was looking for. "I like being friends with you, Vrok."

With our bears in hand, we left the gaming area and strolled through the other events, watching a few rides where monsters, humans, and children of various species shrieked with excitement. We ended up at a stand offering treats.

A sweet, spicy scent clung to the air, and I sucked it in, savoring how amazing it smelled.

"What is that smell?" I asked.

"Funnel cakes. Let's split one."

We purchased the thin, fried item, and Seyla covered the top with a white crystal coating containing brown specks.

"We haven't ruined it with that, have we?" I asked with concern.

"You're going to love it." She led me to a wooden table, and we sat beside each other, the funnel cake on a paper plate between us. "Dig in."

"How does one eat it?" I asked, unsure I was going to enjoy it.

"Break off a piece like this." She demonstrated, wiggling on her seat as she savored the treat. "It's amazing." Her eyes popped open, and she smiled. "Come on. Give it a chance."

She fed Merith a bit, and my dragonette cooed, stretching his neck out, seeking more.

"Only a little, sweetie," she said.

He huffed and shot fake flames into the air, making Seyla's eyes widen.

"I didn't know he could do that," she said with a grin.

"His flames, thankfully, are harmless." I broke a tiny piece off the side of the crispy cake and lifted it to my mouth, smelling it first. The scent was encouraging, hinting at what I'd savored in the air.

I placed it in my mouth, planning to spit it out if it wasn't good, but amazement filled me.

I quickly chewed and swallowed, then broke off a larger section.

"Good, huh?" she said, leaning into my side.

"It really is."

I loved being close to her. I loved spending time with her.

If only I knew whether my feelings were real or generated by the bond.

"Are you sure you want to ride the troller coaster with me?" Seyla asked, her big eyes taking in everything.

"I love roller coasters." Though I'd only ridden one. "Monsters have amusement parks too. This one is one of ours."

"For a while, I kept a log of each I'd ridden, but I'm not sure where it is now. I lost track of a bunch of stuff while moving here and then relocating from Violet and Goreg's B&B to my own place. But I haven't finished unpacking yet. I'm sure it'll turn up."

We purchased a string of tickets we could use on various rides and with them inside my pocket, got in line for the troller coaster.

"What do you think, Merith?" I asked my dragonette. "Ride or not?"

Merith shot me a look of scorn and took flight, soaring over the amusement park before swooping toward where I'd parked my truck.

"Where's he going?" Seyla asked, staring after him.

"I suspect he'll either meet us at home or he'll be sitting on my truck when we're done. I should've suggested he stay home, but he would've protested."

"He doesn't understand when you talk to him, does he?"

"He's smart. Sometimes, it's uncanny how he seems to know what I'm saying."

"Is that common in dragonettes?" she asked.

"It is. In the past, it was common for dragonettes to advise rulers."

"They can't speak."

"They could back then."

"That's amazing," she breathed.

I waved toward the line forming for the roller coaster. "Shall we? It looks rather basic for someone who kept a log of roller coasters you've taken on and defeated." I was tempted to hold her hand. This felt like a real date, and I supposed it was. Would she welcome something like that?

The bond would ensure she did. I didn't like that everything felt forced, even our emotions.

It would be good to end this. Then we could go back to who we were before we met.

"I don't mind that it's a simpler one," Seyla said, her eyes only for me.

I enjoyed being the sole focus of her attention. Guys strolled past us, their gazes locking on her. She had a magical way about her that drew every eye in the place. Much like Margie, someone I hadn't thought about for a while. In fact, I found it hard to believe I'd ever cared for the other woman.

Was that the bond speaking too?

When it was our turn, we climbed into a car, dropping down onto the metal seat. A troll locked a bar in place across the front.

"I feel like I'm three," Seyla said with a laugh, poking the bar that rested against her upper chest. On me, it hit my belly. "I can barely see over the side."

"You could sit on my lap."

She frowned at me. "They won't allow that, will they?"

I pointed to the car ahead of ours, though she might not be able to see over the high back. "Others are doing it."

Her frown remained. "You'd be okay with it?"

"Of course. As Tylik and Raze said, we should make

sure this is what we want, right? How are we going to do that if we keep pretending we're two casual friends?"

"Isn't that your ultimate goal here?"

"Our goal, right?"

She pinched her lips together. "Sure. *Our* goal."

She wanted out of this, didn't she?

CHAPTER 18
SEYLA

Unbuckling, I clambered up onto Vrok's lap. He secured the fastening around us both and made sure the bar remained locked in place.

In all honesty, I liked sitting close to him. It felt right.

But that had to be the bond speaking, which was a big disappointment. I didn't like that I couldn't trust my feelings, that all of this could be something generated by a chemical reaction.

The ride jerked forward. It reached the start of the track, and things smoothed out. Ahead, we'd climb a steep slope, then soar down the other side. From what I saw on the ground, each peak was higher than the last until we reached the final one on top of a giant troll's head. From there, we'd swoop down almost to the ground then climb a few more lower hills before the ride finished.

Vrok's arms went around me, holding against his

muscular frame. "You'll need to hold still," he said in a tight voice.

"I don't think I'll fall." Just in case, I latched onto his forearms. I loved them. As far as forearms went, they were amazing. Made up of green orc skin with a light dusting of hair; they were as muscular as the rest of him. I could sit on the sofa and stare at his arms for hours.

"I'd never let you fall," he vowed as we started our ascent. "It's just . . ."

"You're getting a hard-on." I could feel it nudging my butt, and that was as amazing as his forearms. "We're seeing how this goes between us, correct?"

"Correct," he bit out as the ride continued climbing, the tick-tick-tick of the wheels on the rails echoing around us.

"I can turn around and face you."

"Only if you want to," he snarled.

I loved it when he was grumpy and growly. The sound thrilled through my veins like a shot of the best caffeine.

Did I want to turn? More than anything.

I scrambled around, somehow remaining belted and without the bar doing too much damage to my backside. When I faced him, I braced my legs on either side of his thighs.

He was comically taller than me, so there was no way I could kiss him without his help, but that might be for the best. Somehow, grinding against him felt less intimate than his kisses. When we kissed, I felt like our souls braided together.

His fingertips traced up and down my sides before they slid under my dress.

Good thing the cars were evenly spaced out, and the backs were high to accommodate tall monsters. I couldn't see anything in the cars behind or in front of us. We were alone in our own little world.

He watched my face as his claws glided across my nipples.

The car reached the top of the first peak, and we swooped down the other side. I squealed with excitement that was only partly due to the ride. My mind and body were more focused on the ride I was taking with Vrok.

I tipped my head back and savored the feel of his hands on my breasts.

His stiff cock pressed against his pants, and as tempted as I was to free it, to touch it and see if I could scrunch myself down enough to lick it, the last thing I wanted was for the ride to end with me sucking him off.

I rubbed against him, and he groaned.

He tipped his head back. His fingers went feverish on my breasts, though one slipped out from beneath my dress, gliding around to cup my ass.

When I tilted myself toward him, rocking against his cock, he pushed my ass, adding to the pressure.

In no time, I was writhing on his lap, a panting wreck with only one goal in mind.

As the roller coaster clicked toward the top of the last peak, I rubbed harder against Vrok.

He pinched my nipple, rolling it, and heat blasted through me.

"I'm going to cum," I whispered.

"Do it. Fall apart, Seyla. I'm going to watch."

"You're going to cum too."

"And saturate the front of my pants?" He chuckled, low and husky. "Orcs have tons of cum."

I'd seen.

"You'll be stiff and aching," I said, unable to resist pushing hard against him.

"I'll be a happy orc because I'll know you're completely satisfied. Show me how good I make you feel."

I didn't need more than that.

As the rollercoaster took us along the final loops of the course, I pushed against him.

I came as the ride started to slow, shuddering in my mate's arms.

VROK

The next morning, I strode over to Seyla's house and knocked on her door.

"Oh, hey," she said when she opened it. "Fancy seeing you here."

"We have to decide what we're going to do. Is it alright for me to come in?"

At her nod, I entered, noting how similar the floor plans for our houses were. Most of the buildings on this street had been constructed when a mill was in operation about a hundred years ago.

I dropped onto her sofa, and she perched on a chair opposite me. Her laptop sat open on the table between us, and from the look of it, she had a document open.

Sriracha lounged in another chair. He looked at me, blinking slowly, before returning to his cat nap.

"How's the book coming along?" I asked.

She shrugged. "Good. I'm almost done editing. I'll send it to readers soon and get opinions. If it needs changes, I'll make them before it goes to my proofreader."

"You said you make a living doing this."

"A very good living. Best of all, I love writing." She gave me a soft smile. "I can make the story come out the way I want."

"How does this one end?"

"Like I said, they all have a happy ever after." Shadows skirted across her face. "That makes the best story in the world, doesn't it?"

"What about us, Seyla? What do you want to do?"

"I'll do whatever you want."

"I want us to decide this together."

"It's not easy," she said sadly. "I know how I feel." Her fist pressed against her chest, rubbing.

"I could love you," I said. I suspected I already did. "But would it be real?" I held up my arms, studying the symbols. Even now, chemicals churned through my veins, urging me to be with her fully, to plant my seeds and watch them come to fruition. The drive was older than time.

"I feel the same," she said. "Even now, I want to crawl onto your lap and kiss you. No, I want to strip all my clothes off and drag you to bed. We'd stay there forever." She huffed. "But you're right. Would it be real?"

"I think we should break it." A sad feeling of finality swept over me. Was I making a big mistake?

"So much of me says I shouldn't agree with you."

"Same. Do we have any choice?"

She sighed. "We always have a choice. We could let this rule us. We'd have a happy ever after."

"We'd always know it might not be real."

She stood. "Which is why we need to call Raze and tell him we had a nice night together. We've talked, and we still want to proceed with the spell."

CHAPTER 20
SEYLA

The next day, as the sun was setting, we left Merith at Vrok's house and met Raze at the park. Raze had told us the spell would work best once the sun had set and that it must be performed over water.

"Over there," Raze said, pointing toward a bridge spanning the river. He carried two big bags, and I was curious to see what he'd brought.

We passed a few families packing up after spending the day in the sunshine. A centaur waved, and I waved back while his son trotted over to walk beside us.

"Whatcha doin?" he asked, frowning at Raze's bags.

"We're going to take some pictures of the river at sunset," I said. "It'll be pretty, don't you think?"

The boy stared toward the water glistening in the distance. "It will."

"Come on, Trivarn," the father called. "Time to go."

"Aw," Trivarn shouted. "Can't I stay longer? They're going to take pictures."

Not really, but how could I tell a little boy we were here to perform an orc divorce?

My heart kept tightening at the thought. Everything inside me told me not to do this, to fight for us, but how could I? I wasn't sure what was us and what was the bond feeding our emotions.

It was going to hurt when I didn't love Vrok any longer. I'd taken joy in the emotion, riding it with a smile on my face.

I *liked* him. I wanted to be with him always.

I wanted to ask him to give me children.

Sweat coiled down my spine as the centaur child waved and trotted back to his family. The dad hefted a big picnic basket, then he and his wonderful family broke into a gallop, sweeping across the open field between the picnic area and the parking lot.

Curiosity made me pause to watch. Did they drive cars like humans and most monsters?

This family didn't, at least not for a visit to the park. They slowed their pace when they reached the road and continued on the sidewalk, aiming for the center of town.

A glance around showed me the sun hovered on the horizon and everyone else had left the park.

"We'll set things up in the center of the bridge," Raze said, urging us up onto the wooden structure spanning the river. "I'll need to strip to just a loincloth." He flashed me a smile. "Hope that's okay. Most spells require the performer to be naked, but I've found they work alright as long as I'm not wearing much."

"It's fine," I bit out, my skin crawling with discomfort, though not because Raze would strip. My heart thudded faster than it should, and my palms had gone sweaty solely because of what we were about to do.

We stopped in the middle of the bridge.

Raze dropped the bags onto the wooden surface, and something clanged inside one of them.

"This is improvised, of course," he said, pulling a round piece of metal from the bag that looked a bit like a big wok. He dropped it on the center of the wooden surface, then added bits of fluff and sticks. "I need to light a small fire. Tylik has provided all the ingredients, however, and it's a fairly simple spell. This shouldn't take long." He pulled small jars and a few paper packets from the second bag, placing them on the wooden bridge but away from the fire.

"First," he said. "Pale blue candles to purify the area." He lit three and placed them in a circle around his improvised firepit. He tapped one ingredient after another. "Three grains of fairy dust."

They sparkled like tiny fireflies inside the clear jar with a cork stopper.

"Five strands of cougar shifter fur."

The golden hairs lay inside a small clear paper packet.

"Unicorn horn dust, properly obtained from a deceased elder. Their youngest offspring is usually entrusted to grind the horn and process it for spells. If it was stolen or forced, it wouldn't work." The powder had been placed in a bright golden box that appeared to be made of metal. Was it real gold?

Good thing he trusted Tylik to get only humanely obtained ingredients.

"Only one left," Raze said, tapping a tall, thin vial lying on its side. "A phoenix feather. You can probably thank your friend Nyxor for that. When he sheds, he collects them and gives them to Tylik."

The candles flared, and I caught a whiff of something that smelled vaguely like peppermint, only with a sharp, almost earthy follow up. It filled the air, almost coating it, and subtle whispers echoed around us.

"Is it okay to speak while you're doing this?" I asked.

"If you have questions," Raze said. "You should ask them now. I'd rather you didn't talk while I'm performing the final parts of the spell." His somber gaze caught mine. "Please know you may see or hear things that to a human will feel unworldly, but they're only part of the spell."

"What sort of things?"

He shrugged. "I've never done this spell before, so I can't truly say. It's common for a spirit to be summoned to aide me in the spell, and it may be a creature or a monster like me. Or maybe no creature will participate. We'll know soon."

"I promise I'll be quiet."

Vrok took my hand and squeezed it. We leaned against the opposite rail, watching Raze remove all his clothing other than a strip of leather wound around his waist and between his legs, barely covering the vital areas.

Funny. A gorgeous ogre had removed almost all of his clothing, but my pulse didn't skip even one beat. Vrok was the only one I wanted to see naked.

"Once the spell is concluded, will we see instant results?" I asked.

"If it works, yes."

"It may not work?" Vrok asked.

Raze shrugged. "Like I said. I've never performed this before, but I trust Tylik. He's the expert. I'll follow the directions explicitly. You two should be divorced within minutes."

I traced my fingers across one of the vine patterns. I'd miss them when they were gone.

I'd miss Vrok.

No, that wasn't right. I'd still see him. We'd be friends. Maybe once the bond was broken, he'd visit occasionally to help me with my books.

"I'm going to begin now," Raze said, his solemn gaze first meeting mine, and then Vrok's. "You're completely sure you want to do this?"

Pinching my eyes shut, I jerked out a nod. I couldn't speak; it would hurt too much if I did.

Vrok murmured an agreement.

"Very well," Raze said sadly. "Please remain silent."

CHAPTER 21
VROK

Raze slowly danced around the fire, mumbling words in the ancient ogre tongue. I couldn't understand, but that was okay. I wasn't sure I wanted to know.

I kept thinking about what would happen once our mate bond is over. Would I still crave Seyla, or would I look at her and wonder why I'd been so eager to lick every inch of her body?

Her hand was sweaty in mine, but that was okay too. I kept swiping away the beads of sweat trickling down my forehead.

Pausing, Raze lifted the vial of fairy dust. He opened it with the cork facing down, over the fire, and the three specks floated out and onto the flames. They blazed and Raze flung himself backward. He crouched, watching until the flames died back down.

With a nod, he lifted a small wooden bowl, placing it within the circle created by the three candles. In it, he dumped the unicorn horn dust, adding the cougar fur and finally draping the phoenix feather across the top of the mix.

He upended wax from the candles into the bowl, one after the other, and a strong smell blasted through the air, making my hair fly out behind me.

Seyla looked up at me with concern, and I'd never seen anyone prettier than this woman bathed in firelight.

Was I making a horrible mistake?

This was how it needed to be, but were we wrong to break something gifted to us by the fates?

It was too late now. We'd committed to seeing this through, and the fates help us if we had regrets in the morning.

"Break this bond so they may be free," Raze said. "No more perfect love their paths shall see."

Lifting the phoenix feather, he lit it aflame on the closest candle. Quickly, he touched the blazing tip on each of the other candles before dropping it into the firepit.

He leaned back on his haunches as smoke swirled up from the fire, reaching toward the clouds and blasting past them.

The spiral of smoke winked out, as did the fire, leaving us alone in silence only broken by our ragged breathing.

"Done," Raze said, his voice full of sorrow. "I have a flashlight in my bag. Let me grab it, and we'll take a look."

Seyla squeezed my hand, and I returned the gesture.

I wasn't sure how I felt, but I'd know soon.

Raze clicked on the light and directed it toward us.

Seyla gasped.

The symbols remained on our wrists.

CHAPTER 22

SEYLA

I ran my fingers across the symbol on my right wrist, but in my heart, I already knew.

We were still bonded.

"I did everything correctly. I know that," Raze said. "But for some reason, the spell didn't take." His gaze sought mine, then Vrok's. "I could do it again if you'd like."

"Is there a chance the second spell could work when the first hasn't?" Vrok asked.

Raze shook his head. "I doubt it."

At my nod, he started picking up his supplies.

"What should we do?" I asked.

He carried the dregs of the fire over to the bank and dumped them in the mud, then returned to stuff the metal pan into a bag. "I suggest you escalate this."

"What do you mean?" Vrok asked.

"My mother can perform a stronger spell. She'll have to do it on the cusp of the veil leading to the fae realm, however, since what she'll do is strictly forbidden by the treaty."

What would it entail? It appeared I was going to find out.

"Then that's what we'll do," Vrok said, his gaze seeking mine. "Right?"

"Yup." My mouth tightened and my belly churned. I wasn't sure how I felt.

Actually, I felt good, like things were going the way they were supposed to. It had to be the bond speaking, however, not my heart.

"I'll reach out to Mom," Raze said as we helped him carry everything to his vehicle. "Expect to hear from her soon."

Vrok and I said nothing as we drove home. By the time he'd parked in his driveway, he'd received a text message from Raze.

Mom will pick you two up late tomorrow afternoon. Pack a bag for at least one night.

"Do you know anything about what she'll do?" I asked Vrok as we sat in his driveway.

He shook his head, turning off his truck. "Not in the least. I've scoured the internet, but monsters are still leery about posting information where humans could find it. I could barely learn much about the bond to begin with. Rylee has a blog, and she posts every few months, but she tends to focus on her relationship with Gunner and Josh, their son. I haven't had the heart to ask Max."

"Do you want to do something together before we

leave?" I was clinging, but I couldn't seem to help myself. I wanted to be with him always. Was that so bad?

"I have to catch up on work if I'm going to be gone for a few days." He stared forward, not meeting my eyes.

"Alright, then." I opened my door. "I'll see you tomorrow afternoon when Annalisa gets here."

I took the time to finish editing my book, but I kept stalling with the ending. Nothing felt right.

Like me and Vrok.

I put it aside. Maybe once the bond was broken, I'd find a way to give my couple the happy ending they deserved.

After that, I started plotting the next book in a different series, a monster novella about a woman and a gargoyle. I wanted to write something fun and light-hearted, but my heart kept pinching as I typed their first meet up.

Sriracha kept trying to help, flopping on my keyboard and looking up at me, telling me with purrs and soft meows that my sole priority in life should be stroking him.

Numerous pats and scratches beneath his chin resulted in cat hair flying everywhere, too much of it landing in my coffee.

Eventually, I put the story away and doom scrolled on the internet.

Late afternoon, I took Sriracha to Luna's pet boarding place and dropped him off.

"I'm sorry I can't give you an exact time of pick-up," I told her.

"It's fine," she said with a smile. "He's a sweetie. I'm happy to have him. You know I'm open all the time. Pets are my thing. I promise to give him lots of love and pats. He'll barely miss you."

"Thanks." I wanted to ask her about mating bonds. Did she think those bonded ever doubted it was real? I just wasn't sure what I thought about all this.

I returned home and double checked my bag, dropping it by the front door.

When a tinkling sound rang out from the front of my house, I peered out the front door, taking in the elf carriage pulled by four flisteers, which vaguely resembled unicorns with wings. They were borrowed from the fae realm, brought here by elves.

I'd ridden in a carriage like this before with Kate and Tylik, watching out the windows as the flisteers pulled us through the air.

Annalisa stood beside the carriage. When she caught my eye, she waved.

I grabbed my bag and stepped onto my small front deck, locking the front door behind me.

Vrok came outside. Merith left his shoulder and flew over to land on mine. I stroked his gorgeous spine, and he purred as I walked over to Annalisa's vehicle.

Vrok and I put our bags in the back of the carriage and climbed inside.

I was surprised to see Murtik seated opposite me and Vrok, but maybe he and Annalisa had patched things up. Last I'd heard, they were arguing—with good reason. Murtik tended to flirt, something that would drive me out of my mind if I were dating him.

Merith hopped off my shoulder to sit between me and Vrok. He seemed to frown at me, then Vrok, but what did I know about dragonettes?

"All set?" Annalisa asked, climbing inside and settling beside Murtik. He placed his big palm on her thigh, squeezing gently.

"Yup," me and Vrok said at the same time.

The symbols on my wrists flared now that I was near him, and I noticed his doing the same thing. I'd become used to them. I *liked* seeing them. It was going to be strange when they disappeared.

"What can we expect from this?" I asked.

"It'll take a few hours to reach the edge of the veil," Annalisa said. "We'll spend the night there. I've made arrangements for rooms for us." Her gaze went from me to Vrok. "As for the spell, it's best if I don't share too many details. As my son mentioned, castings like this are strictly forbidden within the human realm. I've received permission to perform it. However, I had to promise I'd do so on the cusp between the fae and human realms where such things are allowed."

She leaned against Murtik, and he put a wing around her back. "Are you sure you want to do this? A mating bond is sacred. Breaking it . . ." She shook her head sadly. "If you have regrets, there will be no turning back."

"What regrets could we have?" Vrok asked. "This was forced upon us. We don't know what's real and what isn't."

"If you want to be with each other, it's real. Trust me." She stroked Murtik's thigh, and he kissed her temple. "Unless you two dislike each other?"

Vrok and I looked at each other.

"I like him," I said softly. I suspected I always would, bond or no bond.

"I feel the same," he said with a smile just for me.

Annalisa huffed out a breath. "And yet you still want me to do this?"

"Yes," Vrok and I said at the same time.

If pressed, I'd have to admit that I didn't want to end it, but the thought of forcing Vrok to be with me when deep inside, he didn't want to share my life, was like a big boot stomping on my emotions. Love should be freely given.

"Alright, then," she said, tapping the wall of the carriage.

The carriage took off, soaring over the town and forest. We'd only traveled for ten minutes or so before an odd sound rang out behind us.

"There's no traffic up here, is there?" I asked, scooting forward on my seat to look out the window, though I saw nothing.

"I haven't flown via carriage since I left the fae realm, but it's rare to see another vehicle in the sky," Annalisa said.

"I only see fellow gargoyles, plus a few dragons and

wyverns," Murtik said with a frown. His hand twitched at his side where he wore a blade strapped to his belt. "I'll investigate."

He opened the door and leapt outward. His wings snapped wide as the carriage passed him.

Vrok growled as the odd sound grew louder. It finally occurred to me what I was hearing.

"A police siren?" I asked, frowning. When I ducked my head out through the window opening again, I gulped to see a cop vehicle approaching behind us, its lights flashing. I slunk into my seat. "Sheriff Venom's pulling us over. Is that even possible when we're flying? He's . . . driving an SUV, which should not be soaring through the sky."

"I haven't heard of our demon friend doing anything like this before," Annalisa said.

"Were we speeding?" I asked inanely.

"I don't believe such a thing can happen with flisteers," Vrok said. "They have one pace."

The carriage slowed, and I worried it would drop from the sky if the flisteers stopped flapping their wings. I'd already learned from Tylik that the carriage itself was suspended behind the creatures by magic. Kind of like the mythical Santa riding in his sleigh pulled by eight reindeer. They directed it; they didn't hold it up in the air. Still, it was a disconcerting thought.

The siren cut out, and Murtik rejoined us inside the carriage.

"Venom has a few questions," he said, settling in the

seat beside Annalisa. "He says this is a routine traffic stop."

Vrok and I blinked at each other.

Sheriff Venom soon hovered outside the left window, peering into the carriage.

"Where are you going at this time of night?" he asked. His reddish bronze skin gleamed in the late-day sunshine. He resembled every mythical demon I'd seen in books, with thick horns jutting up from his forehead and across his head, and dark hair. His muscular build rivaled that of an orc or ogre, stretching the fabric of his sheriff's uniform. I'd heard he could sometimes perform magic.

"I have a spell to perform," Annalisa said with a lift of her dark eyebrows. "If you'll be so kind as to allow us to proceed, Venom."

"What kind of spell?" he asked, nodding to me and Vrok. "You know most of them are forbidden."

"I have special permission to perform a mating bond break spell," she said.

"Who in hell would want to break a mating bond?" he barked, his fiery glare shooting me and Vrok's way again. His gaze fell on our wrists, and he grumbled. "You two?"

"Yes," Vrok said tightly.

"There was a time when I would've killed—and may have done so—to hold onto my fated mate," he said. "I can't believe anyone would be willing to ruin something so precious."

I hadn't heard that demons mated, but I didn't know

much about them. Our sheriff was the only one around. No one was quite sure how he'd ended up in Monsterville running for sheriff, and no one dared ask him. Tylik eluded that Venom had left the underworld and didn't plan to return. I supposed the underworld was the same thing as hell.

"We feel differently," Vrok said carefully.

"But she's the light to your darkness," Venom growled, his poetic words coming out with a snarl would be comical under any other circumstances.

Vrok winced. "I'm an orc, not a demon. I don't possess darkness."

"That's what so many have said before you." Venom shook his head. "You know what I mean."

I didn't, and I assumed Vrok didn't either.

Annalisa watched us. "Do you need any further information from us?" She held out her hand, palm up, and a gleaming gold star appeared on her calloused skin. "This is my pass. We'll travel to the border, where we'll stay until the spell has been completed tomorrow or the next day, depending on the weather. It needs to be clear for me to perform the spell."

Sheriff Venom grumbled. "No, I don't have any further questions." He flicked his claws our way. "Go, you fools. But know right now that you're making a terrible, irrevocable mistake." Sorrow filled his dark eyes, the flames extinguished. "If I could have even one moment with *her*, I'd never waste it."

Who was he talking about? I didn't dare ask.

From the way Annalisa and Murtik's lips tightened, they must feel the same.

Turning, our sheriff floated back to his vehicle.

I watched as the SUV soared down toward a road far beneath us. The vehicle hit the pavement, turned, and headed back toward town.

"Our delightful sheriff just delivered interesting information," Annalisa said softly. Her gaze met Murtik's, and he nodded.

The carriage flew a few hours before it started slowing, then landed in a huge field. The sun had long since left the world, but lights strung around the outer aspect of the open area invited us to step outside and approach them.

Five gleaming silver buildings resembling small castles unlike anything I'd seen before stood along one side of the field in a row. Beyond them, I swore the air wavered. The veil between my world and the fae realm? It must be.

The vehicle pulled up to the front of one of the castles, and we got out, grabbing our bags from the back.

Merith settled on Vrok's right shoulder.

"This way," Annalisa said, striding toward the building. We went inside, and I gawked at the silver etching along the ceiling and around the doorways of the big open foyer. "There are two bedrooms in this building." Her gaze fell on us. "Murtik and I will take one and you may have the other."

CHAPTER 23

VROK

"We're here to break our mating bond and you want us to sleep together?" I asked, keeping my voice as neutral as possible.

My heart leapt at the thought when it shouldn't have. Would I feel differently when this was over? It would be strange to look at Seyla and feel nothing.

"We can't sleep together," Seyla said, sidling close to my side.

I put my arm around her, tugging her near.

"I obtained these rooms on short notice," Annalisa said. "There are no others in the area."

"We could sleep outside," Seyla said, looking up at me. "Or somewhere else inside the building. Whatever."

"If we sleep together, we'll solidify the bond," I pointed out.

My insides had been churning since we left Monster-ville. Venom's words had only deepened my growing dismay.

Did I truly want to end the bond with Seyla? All I could picture was the bliss on her face when she ground herself against me while we rode the troller coaster. The way she'd teased me in the kitchen, reciting lines from her book. And how Merith adored her.

Was I making the biggest mistake of my life?

I was tempted to call an end to this, but it wasn't solely about me. Seyla wanted out and pushing her to stay bonded with me against her will would be an even bigger mistake than ending it.

"What makes you think the bond will solidify if you're together?" Annalisa asked.

"We haven't . . . had penetration," I said. "The bond is there, but it's not complete yet."

Annalisa snorted. "That's an old tale that's not based on fact."

"You mean if we have sex, we won't deepen the bond?" Seyla asked with a frown.

"That's correct," Annalisa said.

Seyla shot an uncertain glance my way. "Huh."

"What would you like to do?" I asked.

She shrugged. "We can share. It'll be okay. We don't . . . have to do anything."

"Very well," Annalisa said. "Murtik and I will see you at dawn. If the sun shines and there's no rain in the forecast, I'll proceed with the spell. Do not eat after midnight, please. The spell will work best if your bellies are empty."

We took our bags up the stairs, finding a landing that

split to the left and right. A solitary door waited on each side.

"This way," Annalisa told Murtik. Her solemn glance fell on us. "You two have the other suite."

We entered, shutting the door behind us, and I took in the enormous living area. Arched doorways exited on our left and right.

Merith left my shoulder, soaring over to land on the back of the sofa. He watched us, but like most of my pet's expressions, I couldn't interpret what he might be thinking. Probably wondering where we were and why we'd come here. Nothing more than that.

Seyla paced across the room to the right, and I followed.

"Kitchen," she said, stepping inside and opening the refrigerator. "Stocked if we want a snack before midnight."

I followed her to the other open doorway, where we found a big room with a bed large enough to accommodate many oversized monsters.

"Double orc-sized," she said. "I can take the couch if you want."

"Or I can."

"Or . . ." She turned fully to face me. "We could share the bed."

My pulse jumped. "What are you saying, Seyla?"

"I have a favor to ask." Her gaze fled mine, down to her hands clamped tightly together in front of her body. "Would you make love to me?"

I gulped, unsure of what to say.

She held up a finger, her gaze meeting mine. "Let me explain. See, I'm in love with you. I know it's not real, but this may be the only time I'll love anyone as much as this. After tomorrow, it'll be gone." Her penetrating gaze met mine. "I want to know what it's like to be with someone I love, someone I'd die for, someone I'd sacrifice anything to make happy. That's you, Vrok, for better or for worse." Her swallow took a long time going down. "If you don't want to do this, I understand. Say no, then, but I wanted to ask."

"I want that more than anything, Seyla," I said, my voice breaking. "I also want to know what it feels like to be with someone I love."

He shut the bedroom door and stepped toward me.

I met him halfway.

Holding hands, we stared at each other for a long while.

"It's funny," I said.

"What?" Releasing one of my hands, he stroked the hair off my face, brushing it past my shoulder.

Even such a simple touch burned through me like the hottest fire. It ignited something inside me, a craving for Vrok I couldn't deny.

"Each time we've done something sexual, it's been spontaneous," I said. "And from my side of the equation, it felt like we couldn't hold ourselves back. Now we're in a bedroom and we're going to do everything, but I feel shy."

"We don't have to do anything if you don't want to."

My laugh popped out a bit too high pitched for my comfort. "Oh, I want to do it. I have for a long time."

"It's been the same for me. I did my best to keep from feeling anything for you. I was hurt, and I didn't want to be wounded again. I suspected from the start that the blow you could deal me would be ten times worse than the one I'd received from my ex."

"And now, here we are, about to have sex. In the morning, we'll end our bond and go our separate ways. I won't crave you and you won't long for me." The thought of not being with him made me want to curl up in a ball and cry. Would that feeling leave me as well? It better.

"We can go slowly, then."

I grinned. "Until things catch up with us and sweep us away."

His grin matched mine. "I have a feeling it won't take us long." He grabbed the hem of his shirt and tugged it over his head. It snagged on his horns, and he growled as he wrangled with it.

"Let me help," I said.

He stooped forward, and I carefully tugged the fabric away from his horns, easing the shirt over his head.

"You've got a great body," I said, admiring his muscular chest.

"So do you," he said, his fingertips teasing beneath my shirt, across my belly. "Show it to me. I want to suck on everything."

"You do well with sucking."

A devilish smile tugged at the corners of his mouth. "I'm inspired when I'm with you."

I ripped my shirt off and then my bra.

"Gorgeous breasts with big dark nipples in need of sucking," he said, bending forward. He licked one nipple while his fingers traced across the other, making each form tight buds.

I was immediately overwhelmed with sensation. My head tipped back, and I moaned at the heady, wondrous feeling of him loving my breasts.

He undid my pants, and I shimmied my hips to get rid of them. My panties too.

In no time, I'd undone his pants, and he'd removed them. Throughout our awkward movements, he maintained a tight suction on my nipple with his mouth.

His claws traced down my sides and across my hips to my ass, which he gripped, pulling me fully against him.

He had a hard-on already, and I gripped the thick, long thing, stroking it while he moaned against my breast.

Leaving my nipple with a wet pop, he kissed up across my neck until he could claim my mouth.

His tongue stroked mine, tangling us together until I wasn't sure where he began, and I ended.

Everywhere. I didn't end; this was just the beginning.

Fated one, my heart cried. We were perfection. Wonder. Beauty. There would never be another who could replace him.

He lifted me and carried me over to the bed, laying me on the silky blanket. It felt amazing against my bare skin, but him crawling over me, surrounding me, felt even better.

He continued kissing me, and I stroked his horns, marveling at how different yet similar we were. We were two colliding souls finding joy with each other.

Tomorrow, we'd end it.

I didn't want to think about that. I had tonight to savor, to bring me to life.

He stroked down my thigh, and I parted my legs. His fingertips found me, caressed me, and in no time, I writhed beneath him, begging for everything with feral whimpers.

"Not so fast," he murmured, kissing my breasts and sucking on my nipples. He kissed downward, across my belly, and plunged his tongue inside me, swirling it. The pad of his thumb centered on my clit, stroking until I couldn't tell where he began, and I finished.

I bucked up toward him, and he braced me with one arm, pinning me to the bed.

An orgasm rocked through me, and I shrieked, my cries dissolving into moans. The strokes of his tongue slowed, and he carefully licked my inner walls, groaning.

I didn't think my body could handle more, but soon, his soft touch deepened, and he added a finger inside me, gliding it back and forth across my G-Spot.

A moan wrenched from me, and he looked up, his eyes sparkling.

He drew his tongue out and rose above me. "I need you."

"I'm yours, Vrok. I love you."

"And I love you." Rolling me over, he hitched my hips up, spreading my legs wide.

I bit down on the back of my hand and pressed backward, needing this. Needing him.

He centered his cock at my core.

With a thrust, he pushed himself partway inside me. Damn, it felt good. His girth stretched me almost past the point where I couldn't bear it, but I adored how wonderful it felt to be filled by him.

Pulling out, he held my hips snugly and thrust forward again, seating himself deeper.

"You're with me?" he asked hoarsely, leaning over to kiss the back of my neck. He bit down gently with his tusks, and that drove me higher.

"Always, Vrok." *Always,* my heart cried.

He curled himself forward and kept kissing my neck and shoulders. As his tongue glided across my overheated skin, he pulled out and drove himself deeper, bottoming out deeply. It was too much, yet this moment would never be enough. I was a greedy person, rocking back to meet him, lifting my hips to make sure I didn't miss even an inch of his glorious cock.

Our groans echoed around us as he started to move, alternating his thrusts to reach deep within me while stroking my inner walls as he pulled out.

He moved faster, and his hand slid underneath me. He captured my clit as he did everything inside me, and I lost all focus.

Everything I was would be tied up in him for the rest of my life. Somehow, I knew this.

In this perfect moment, as he moved faster, his groans merging with my panting pleas for more and faster, we became one.

Our bodies gave way to bliss, riding it until it had spent itself on a sandy shore.

CHAPTER 25
VROK

Unable to get enough of Seyla, I loved her all night. I took her from behind again, while we spooned together, from the front, and as dawn began to peek above the horizon, I dragged her from bed and lifted her, pressing her against the wall.

"Again?" She nudged my arm but kissed my chest.

I nodded.

"Take me hard and fast then. Imprint everything in my mind forever."

That had already happened to me. How was I going to walk away from the best thing in my life?

Seyla, my soul cried, and I struggled to ignore it. It was the bond speaking. No, it was Seyla. She and I were crafting something special, something I sensed I'd never find again with another.

I cupped her face and locked my eyes on hers. I wanted this to be the best and our last, to be everything.

I'd never love her again after this time, and that had to be a crime.

As she clung to me, I moved within her. Her sighs grew louder. She stroked my horns, her heels on my ass driving me to take her harder. Each thrust within her hot core felt like a day, a week, a lifetime of loving.

When she came, her body rippling around mine, I succumbed to the pleasure I sensed I'd only find with this woman.

Wrung out, we trembled together, her back still against the wall, my cock buried deep within her.

She looked up at me and gave me the sweetest smile.

I tumbled back onto the bed, holding her, and she snuggled close, pressing soft kisses on my sweaty flesh.

Until someone knocked on the outer door.

"I'm going downstairs," Annalisa called out. "Please join me within fifteen minutes. Remember, don't eat."

We showered quickly, and while I was tempted to take things further with her, to snatch one more taste of what I'd never savor again, it was time.

As the sun hitched its way up into the sky, we hurried down the stairs and outside.

Annalisa and Murtik waited on the front lawn. She wore a long, pure black gown, and he was dressed in equally black clothing.

Her solemn gaze swept from me to Seyla. "Yes or no?"

I couldn't speak the word. I could only blink.

Seyla squeezed my hand and jerked out a nod.

"Very well then," Annalisa said, nudging her head toward the woods. "If you'll follow me."

Murtik cupped her face and gave her a kiss. "I'll see you when it's over?"

"Please come for me after." She clung to his arms, leaning into his chest. "This is not going to be easy."

"I love you," he whispered. "I'll always be here for you."

"Finally." She smiled at him. "I love you too, Murtik."

"Then do what you must, love. I'll always be here to catch you."

After they kissed, he took flight, soaring up over the castle.

"He cannot be here for this," Annalisa said sadly. She waved toward the side of the castle. "Follow me. I'll take you to the edge of the veil where everything has been laid out in preparation."

We entered the forest.

CHAPTER 26
SEYLA

Annalisa followed a narrow trail deep into the woods, the bag she carried banging against her calf.

Vrok took it from her, shouldering it, and we walked single file behind her.

I kept shooting gazes at him over my shoulder, though I wasn't quite sure why. Did I expect him to pronounce he didn't want the spell after all, that he'd decided during the night that what we had shouldn't be severed?

That's what I wanted to say, but how could I? It wasn't the heartfelt emotions swirling inside me, the ones insisting this was real and not a manifestation of the bond. Deep in my soul, I knew this could be lasting. What we'd shared last night was special. How could that ever be wrong?

But Vrok didn't want the bond. He didn't truly want *me*. The thought of that was ripping me apart.

We emerged into a small, circular grassy meadow with the woods looming around us.

Tiny pink flowers grew in perfusion across the open area, a blanket that gave the setting the feel of a dream or a fairytale.

Annalisa removed her shoes and nodded our way to indicate we should do the same. Her long black dress swished around her ankles as she strode to the center of the meadow, urging us to follow. She took the bag from Vrok and dropped it in the grass, kneeling down to pull things from it.

First, a roughly carved wooden bowl that seemed to glow in the early morning sunlight, like it had a life of its own.

Fae wood?

Slowly and methodically, she began to add ingredients to the bowl, whispering strange words and chanting in a language I didn't understand. First, she added a handful of pungent herbs, their aroma strong and earthy. It enveloped me; it was all I could do not to sneeze. Fascinated, I could barely look away, though I did glance at Vrok.

Was I hoping he'd call a halt to this before she'd finished? His lips remained in a straight line with only a rare twitch across his tusks.

Annalisa continued to murmur, adding a big pinch of something that glittered like stardust. When it drifted over the herbs, they flared, making the inner sides of the bowl sparkle. An odd hum rang out before everything went silent again. If wild creatures happened to be nearby, I sensed they'd flee the area. Not even the chirp of a bird broke through her chanting.

Next, she pulled a vial from the bag and added a single drop on the top of the mix. As it fell from the dropper, it gleamed like an oil slick on a puddle of water. I swore I saw . . . *so much* within the drop, as if it contained a complete world and those there cried out a warning.

Even the mythical beings seemed to be telling me that what we were doing was wrong, that we'd regret this.

I rubbed my arms to eliminate my shivers, but they persisted.

It's not what you're thinking, I told myself. *This has to be done. It's wrong for us to continue a relationship caused by a chemical reaction.*

Finally, she tugged what looked like a piece of wood from the bag, one in a color much different from the bowl. Unlike a random stick, this piece glowed in a rich burgundy almost as red as blood. Smooth and worn like it had been around for ages, it was the length and width of her forearm. She pulled out a simple kitchen grater like I'd use to grind a block of cheese. Holding them both over the bowl, she released five sharp cries, grating down the wood sharply with each call. Bits of the wood drifted over the mix in the bowl, and it started churning all on its own, spinning slowly at first in a counterclockwise direction, then increasing its pace.

The ingredients swirled together like I'd thrown them into a blender, churning the mix into a smooth, glowing liquid.

Annalisa rose from her squat and glided slowly around the bowl in the opposite direction of the flow. Her arms extended and her eyes closed, she chanted, repeating a phrase over and over in a language that sounded older than time.

The liquid sloshed faster, and the color changed from a mossy brown to a bright blue. As she quickened the stomps of her bare feet, the liquid flashed to blood red, then a black darker than the deepest night.

The symbols on my wrists flared and faded, over and over, as did those on Vrok's arms. It stung like a bee when they blazed brightly, but I held in my gasp.

With a sharp cry, Annalisa stopped opposite the bowl from us. Her hands dropped to her sides, and the liquid came to a standstill. So clear, it almost appeared as if there was nothing inside the bowl.

Annalisa bowed her head and released a low stream of words.

Stooping down, she tugged two metal cups from the bag and placed them beside the bowl. Grasping the sides with her wrists, not her fingers, she upended it, pouring half of the liquid into each of the cups.

"Take one," she said dully, not looking our way. "Each of you. Drink it until it is gone, and your will shall be done."

Rising, she bowed. She turned and strode across the meadow.

Murtik appeared at the head of the path. When she staggered, he rushed forward and lifted her into his arms. He kissed her forehead gently and took flight.

Soaring up over the forest, he carried her toward the castles.

Vrok and I split and walked around the bowl. We each took a cup.

I wasn't sure if we could speak, but my eyes met his. Even now, I hoped I'd see something there that would tell me what we should do.

With a deep sigh, he broke our eye contact and lifted his cup. He drained it and a shudder ripped through him.

No, my soul cried.

I ignored it. What else could I do?

I, too, drank the liquid. It tasted like the bitter ashes after a house fire, the desolate emptiness in the heart of a child long abandoned, and the dregs of everything wrong in our world.

When I finished, the cup fell from my hand, thudding on the ground, as did Vrok's.

I felt the sting in my wrists, but my gaze was focused on Vrok. His symbols flared one last time before fading to nothing, leaving him as quickly as they'd arrived.

I released a sharp keen as I lifted my arms, finding only smooth, unmarred skin where so much beauty had found a home.

"It's done," he said dully, slowly walking toward the path, not once glancing my way. "We'll take a carriage home."

Following him, my pulse drummed heavily in my throat.

I stared at his back as we walked through the woods.

No, I memorized his back, the shape of his head, and his light scent drifting around me.

Because I still wanted Vrok. More than anything.

The spell may have stolen our bonding symbols, but I still wanted *him*.

If anything, my love for him had deepened.

CHAPTER 27
VROK

I walked through the woods, hyperaware of Seyla striding behind me.

There was nothing I could say to her, yet I wanted so much to stop on the path. I'd turn and fall to my knees. I'd take her hands.

Then I'd beg her to love me once more.

The spell had removed the bond. I felt it sever within me.

But I still loved her. So much. It's beauty and grace soared through me like the purest song.

Merith cried out from ahead. He soared through the forest, seeking us, the sunlight glinting off his golden scales.

When he reached me, he drew up, his wings flapping, stirring fallen leaves on the ground. He squawked, and I swore he glared. Let him. He couldn't scorn me any more than I did myself.

What had I done?

Actually, I knew what I'd done. I'd severed something precious, something I should've treasured above everything else in my life, solely because I'd doubted true love could come to someone such as me.

I'd doubted us.

Merith flew past me and landed on Seyla's shoulder.

Her glance met mine, and I was stunned by the sadness there. She must be glad that it was over, that she wasn't being forced into a relationship she didn't want.

We'd agreed to do this; now we'd have to live with the result of our actions.

When we approached the castle, an elderly fae woman left the building and walked over to join us on the crushed stone path encircling the big structure.

"Annalisa asked me to pass on a message," she said in a kind voice. Her white-white hair glowed almost silver in the sunlight. She smoothed her hands down her simple blue dress. "She and Murtik have left. He'll return her to her home where she can rest." Her head tilted, and she studied our faces for a long moment before her eyes drifted to Seyla's wrists then mine. "The spell was successful."

"It was," I croaked. I cleared my throat and spoke again. "The mating bond has ended."

Seyla said nothing, just stared at the fae woman blankly.

Merith kept rubbing his face on her cheek, but he didn't purr. He was as unsettled as me.

"I've placed your belongings inside the carriages," the fae woman said, gesturing to two smaller vehicles parked nearby, each pulled by only one flisteer. "I assume you wish to depart now?"

I glanced at Seyla, but she didn't look my way. When she nodded, so did I.

The fae woman's lips twitched. "Very well, then. You may each take a carriage. The flisteers know where to deliver you. I wish you both all the best."

As I climbed into my solitary carriage, and Merith landed on my lap, I had to wonder what the best could be.

I suspected it was last night, when Seyla and I opened our hearts completely to each other.

CHAPTER 28

SEYLA

Kate came by to visit me the next day.

"Hey, girly," she said, sashaying into my living room where I sat on the sofa staring at my laptop. I should open a document and start working on a book, but the thought of writing a happy ever after made my guts lurch.

Sriracha had curled up in the chair opposite the coffee table. He kept giving me sullen looks, my punishment for leaving him at Luna's place for the night. I knew she'd been super sweet to him, but he enjoyed being home the most.

Kate gave him a pat before she dropped onto the sofa and puffed out a breath, making her gorgeous auburn hair flip upward before it settled on the sides of her face. "Man, it's hot out today. We need a solid rain to break up the heat."

I hadn't noticed. I'd slept—somehow—though my dreams had been haunted with images of me and Vrok during our one night together. I woke with tears wetting my face and a heart that was turning into a lump of concrete in my chest. Coming downstairs, I'd staggered into the kitchen, made coffee, and brought it here. It still sat on the table, as stone cold as my soul.

"Tylik and I are going to add a baby's room onto the back of our house," she said.

"That's nice." I stared at my coffee. Had a fruit fly landed in it? Just my luck.

"When the triplets are born, we'll need more room, so we're talking about expanding our hobbit house by more than one room. We'll start there, however. I imagine we can keep them together for a few years at least."

"I understand." Leaning forward, I flicked the fly out of the coffee, though I wouldn't drink it. Damn things just— I frowned. "Triplets? You're pregnant?" I whirled to face her. "Triplets!?"

"Well, we don't know that yet." She smoothed her hand across her belly. "And I'm only guessing I'm pregnant. We haven't been together that long, but . . . I think I'm carrying our baby." Her shy grin was infectious. Why couldn't I get mine to join in? It fell too fast. "What's wrong? You're obviously not listening."

I held up my wrists. I'd already told her about me and Vrok, though I hadn't shared the steamier bits. She'd cheered, stating that now that we were fated mates, he'd never be able to resist me.

He was resisting me quite easily now.

"What happened?" She reached out to touch my

wrist but pulled her finger back as if touching me could be contagious and she'd suddenly feel differently about Tylik. No chance of that. They adored each other, and that wasn't going to change.

I explained about the spell.

"You really wanted to end it?" she said sadly, slumping against my side.

I tipped my head, leaning it on her shoulder. "I had no choice. The feelings were forced."

"Then why are you sad? You should be happy it's over, that you no longer feel pulled in his direction."

"Because I love him," I wailed, new tears springing up in my eyes.

She put her arm around me. "What do you mean?"

"It worked, but it didn't. The symbols are gone. I felt something snap inside me when the spell ended, but my feelings haven't changed. I love him, and I'm going to feel this way until the day I die."

"Why did you do it? Truly?"

"Because it was what Vrok wanted."

"What about what Seyla wanted?"

"I ignored her," I said. "What else could I do?"

"You could've fought for what you two had together." She shook her head and sighed. "Did it ever occur to you that the bond was just one part of what you two shared, that the love you feel couldn't be wiped away like the symbols?"

"I thought the longing would end. I thought we'd be friends after it was over, that we'd cheer each other on as we found new people to be with."

"Aw, Seyla," she said, hugging me. "I'm sorry. What does Vrok say about all this?"

"Absolutely nothing. He seemed fairly happy it was over when he climbed into a carriage. I haven't seen him since, which tells me he's moved on."

"What if . . ." She turned and gave me another bright smile. "What if he's mourning your loss as much as you are him?"

"Wouldn't he have said something?"

"You didn't, did you?"

"Well, no."

"Why not?" she asked with a low laugh.

"I couldn't tell him that I loved him for real, that despite the spell breaking, my feelings hadn't changed."

"You two really messed this up."

"We did," I said. "And I don't think there's any way we can fix it."

"I can ask Tylik if there's a spell to reverse it."

"I thought spells like that were forbidden," I said.

She shrugged. "There's no harm in asking." Rising, she stared down at me with sadness. "I'll let you know what he says. In between then . . ."

"What?" I peered up at her.

"Why don't you do something neighborly for Vrok? It might be a good way to find out if the feelings you're wallowing in are one sided or not."

"There's no chance he still cares." I got up off the sofa and followed her to the front door. "He's probably partying now that it's over." No more craving me or my body. No peering through the fence when I worked in my yard. And no lifting me up onto the kitchen counter to kiss me.

"You made one big mistake," she said. "Why compound it with another?" With that, she opened the front door and reeled backward. "Whoa. Where did the storm come from? The sky was clear when I got here. I better get home."

"Storm?"

"Yeah, the sky's dark and it looks like it's going to pour dogs and cats and centaurs soon."

I squeezed her shoulder. "Drive safe? Please."

"Sure." She sent me a searching look before she left, hurrying to her SUV as it started to sprinkle.

I shut the door and dumped my coffee down the drain. I filled another cup from the pot, adding cream from the fridge. I doubted I'd drink it, but I brought it into the living room just in case.

Lifting my laptop, I opened a document. It was time to start a new story. Maybe the one about gargoyles, because there was no way I could write a romance about orcs.

When thunder rumbled overhead, the lights flickered.

"Looks like a horrible storm, Sriracha," I said to my cat who just blinked at me, tucked his nose into his fluffy tail, and went back to sleep. "It's a storm just like in my last book, the one Vrok helped me with."

My breath caught.

Kate was right—as always.

There *was* something I could do.

CHAPTER 29
VROK

Thunder rumbled overhead, followed by a crack of lightning that lit up the sky.

I sat in my office, trying to work, but between the storm and Merith sending me sullen looks, I wasn't getting anything done. You'd think he'd played matchmaker and fixed me and Seyla up only for me to reject her. Not just reject her but yank her heart from her chest and stomp it flat beneath my shoe.

"I miss her, if it helps," I told him, dropping my pen onto my pile of papers.

He clung to his perch, using the device I'd purchased when I first adopted him. I place him on it when it arrived. He squawked and pecked my hand and he hadn't used it since. It must be okay for today at least.

I sensed he didn't want to come near me, and who could blame him?

"You're right," I said.

I swore he nodded.

"I never should've done it. I should've realized the gift we were given and cherished it. Cherished Seyla."

Now I was convinced he nodded.

My chest hurt. It had ever since I drank Annalisa's potion. I suspected it was going to hurt for the rest of my days.

"The thing is," I told Merith, "we did it because it was what *she* wanted."

He snarled. I'd never heard my dragonette make that sound before.

"She did," I said.

His snarl ripped through the room, and he punctuated it with a sharp glare.

"Okay, maybe she didn't want it. I didn't exactly pin her down and make her tell me what she truly thought. *I* wanted to break it." Why, though? Actually, I didn't need to voice the question. I only needed to spit out the answer. "Margie hurt me, and I was afraid Seyla would do the same thing. To keep it from happening, I shoved her away despite how much I wanted her or how she made me feel."

Merith huffed.

"But she doesn't want me any longer, so maybe it's for the best. It's kinda like she's rejecting me like Margie did, don't you think?"

Merith swooped off his perch and landed on my shoulder. His claws tightened until they almost pierced my skin.

"Hey!" I scrambled out of my seat and spun, trying to pry his claws off before they drew blood.

When his grip eased, I sat in my chair again.

"Okay, you're right," I said. "She wouldn't have rejected me like Margie. She's not the same at all."

She'd loved me. She told me that, and it was true. I felt it in her touch, in her sighs when I loved her, and in the way she looked at me.

This, I knew in my heart.

"She doesn't love me any longer," I said.

Merith pecked my face.

"Stop it," I snapped, though there wasn't much oomph in my voice.

I stared at my desk for a very long time.

"Maybe I should go to Seyla's place. I need to make sure she's okay."

Merith started to purr.

"You like that idea?" I asked.

He nodded.

"I could ask her how she's feeling."

His purr got louder.

"And I can tell her how *I'm* feeling. You're right, buddy. I instigated this. She may not have wanted to end our mating. She might," I pinched my eyes shut, not daring to hope, "she might still love me as much as I do her. I can't let this end without asking."

Merith rubbed his face on my cheek; a sure sign of approval. Taking flight, he soared to the back door. The click of his claws rang out on the glass.

"Right now?" I said, afraid. What if I told her I still wanted her, and she shook her head and said I needed to get lost?

I had a feeling I'd feel much worse than I did when Margie rejected me.

Merith tapped harder on the glass, and I left my office, striding toward the back of the house.

Someone waited on the other side of the door.

Seyla.

CHAPTER 30
SEYLA

"Hey," I said when Vrok opened the door.

Merith soared out and landed on the back lawn, but instead of scratching for bugs, he watched us.

"Hey," Vrok said.

"Is he okay outside in the storm?" I asked, worried about the little dragonette.

"He loves it. He'll tap on the door when he wants to come back inside."

"Alright." Rain slithered down my spine, and I began to think I should turn around and go home. Hide inside for a thousand years. Maybe by then, my heart would stop hurting.

No, I came here for a reason, and I was going to see this through.

I stiffened my spine. "Can I come in for a second?" After showering, I'd tugged on a sundress, needing to feel cute in case my plan went south fast.

I was drenched through from the rain already, water channeling down the back of said pretty dress.

"Of course." He backed away, and I eased past him, holding my breath. If I caught a whiff of his wonderful scent or brushed against him, I was going to cry. After looking outside, he shut the door. "Pretty bad out. Is everything okay at your house?"

"No. Yes. I don't know." My shoulders drooped.

He nodded.

I walked to his kitchen and leaned against the counter. Then, realizing this was the scene of a steamy moment between us, though at my place, I slipped away from the counter and stood beside the doorway to the living room.

"I'm dripping," I said, staring at the pool by my feet. "I'm sorry."

"It's alright, Seyla." He watched me, but I couldn't tell what he was thinking.

"I need help with one final scene in my book," I finally said, my voice shaky. What if this didn't work? What if he rejected me?

Well, then at least I'd know. I could sell my house and move into a new one on the opposite side of the country. I could avoid him. One day, I might even be able to think about him without wanting to curl up and cry.

"What do you need?" he croaked.

Why did he sound as nervous as me?

Maybe he worried us being this close together would trigger the bond again, if such a thing was possible.

"In my book, my couple is at the final, most vital

moment, and I'm afraid if I don't get this right, they'll never find their happy ending." I lifted my phone. "Can I read that section to you and get your opinion on his dialogue?"

"Of course." He took a step toward me, but then froze as if he didn't dare come closer.

Maybe he hated me now. He could believe I took advantage of the situation, and he might be right. I'd wallowed in the feelings growing inside me, wallowed in the mate bond I'd found with him.

Clearing my throat, I started to read. "This is my wyvern speaking."

"You didn't make him an orc."

I just leveled a look at him, daring him to suggest—again—that I change it.

"Wyvern works," he said, scratching the back of his neck. "They're kinda like a dragon, right?"

"You don't know?"

"I'm not an encyclopedia of monsters."

"Okay." I hefted my phone again. Did I dare do this? What if he twisted it around or looked at me with scorn?

I won't know unless I try. I could hear Kate saying that to me.

"What are we going to do? my guy asks," I said.

Vrok nods. At least he's listening.

"Her searching gaze met mine," I read. "And I swore she braced herself."

"What's she bracing herself for?" Vrok asked softly, taking another step toward me.

Did I read caring in his eyes? It could just be the usual neighborly kindness. Or he felt sorry for my couple.

"She's bracing herself for him to tell her she has to leave. Remember? They were trapped inside his house due to a storm."

"It's storming here right now."

Yeah, that was how I came up with the idea.

For a moment, I was scared. This was a fool's errand. I needed to leave.

But I made myself stay, made myself continue.

"In my book, the storm has ended. She knows he's going to tell her he doesn't want her to stay."

"What if he does?" Vrok took another step closer to me.

"He'll have to tell her, which is where I've run into trouble." So much trouble. I was drowning and there was no shore in sight. "He realizes he hasn't told her or really shown her how he truly feels."

Vrok stared at me with so much sorrow it made my breath catch. "How does he feel?"

"He needs to tell her what's in his heart." I gulped and pinched my eyes shut, but blocking Vrok out wouldn't keep him from rejecting me. It would only keep me from seeing the disdain on his face.

"I think he needs to do more than tell her," Vrok said, coming so close to me I could lean forward and brush us together.

He smelled wonderful, like spring rain, the spice you want to rub all over your skin, plus a hint of hope. I clung to the last.

"What should he do in this scene?" I asked, my eyes opened, but still not daring to look up at him.

"I think he should hold her." Vrok took my hand and tugged me into his arms. "Like this."

"Yes, that could work." I was drowning in his touch, though it was oh-so-innocent. He was being nice. A friend. He was helping me act out the scene.

It wasn't real. It wasn't us.

"I know what *I* want to do," he said. "You could write that."

"If I was her, I'd ask him to name it. I'd say, what do you want to do?"

"Well, he'd stroke the tears from her face." Cupping my cheeks gently, he ran his thumbs across mine. They were wet and not only from rain. "He'd hate that he drove her to cry. It would just about kill him."

"What else?" I asked, wishing on every star in the galaxy. *Please, fate, be kind to me.*

"He'd say, I love you, Seyla. Real love, the kind with flowers and romance and him worshiping her every day of her life."

"Her name is Nettie," I croaked out.

"He can tell Nettie he loves her, but as for me, I'm telling Seyla." He held my face, making me look up at him. I saw so much devotion there, the same feelings I'd seen when we were mated. The love I'd seen the one night we were together. "I made such a mistake, Seyla. Why did I throw us away?"

More tears sprung up in my eyes. "You weren't alone in that. I threw you away too. I'm still in love with you,

Vrok. It's real, not anything created by the mating bond. It was always real."

"What are we going to do about it, Seyla?"

"I think you should start by kissing me. We can take it from there."

"Love," he whispered hoarsely.

He lifted me, and his mouth met mine.

And while the storm raged around us, we found each other again.

We found each other for forever.

CHAPTER 31
EPILOGUE
SEYLA

One month later

"Surprise!" I yelled along with our friends.

Kate stood in the doorway of me and Vrok's home. I'd moved in with him, and we were renting my place to the woman I'd met at the fair, Brooke. I'd run into her at Rylee's cupcake shop, and she'd confided she needed a place to stay for a week or so. Violet and Goreg's B&B had no rooms. I'd suggested she come to the shower, but she'd told me she had other plans.

"Is all this for me?" Kate asked, her hand on her barely there belly. She grinned at Tylik standing protectively behind her in the doorway.

"Come inside," Grannie Vi called out, waving her cane. "You're letting the AC out."

"You're right, Vi. So right," Uncle Bub said from beside her on the sofa.

I bustled over to Kate and gave her a hug. "You didn't think you'd get away without a baby shower, now did you?"

"But I'm only a few months pregnant," she said, beaming at everyone. "Aw, this is so sweet."

"You look amazing as always," Chastity said, coming forward to give Kate her second hug of the evening. Max followed with Sydnee on his shoulder. She squirmed, wanting to get down. She'd started pulling herself up while holding onto furniture, and she was getting into everything. I'd have to babyproof our home soon, and not only to protect everything from Sydnee. By next spring, me and Vrok would welcome our first child.

Max put Sydnee down, though he kept a firm grip on the back of her overalls, holding her feet above the floor. Squealing, she moonwalked, trying to get free.

"Have a seat in the spot for the guest of honor, Kate," Vrok said, his arm going around my shoulder. He kissed my forehead before waving to the gaily decorated chair with a banner, *Welcome Baby,* hanging above.

Everyone was here, and my cheeks hurt from grinning.

Luna sat on Storm's lap and Sriracha sat on hers, purring and sending me looks that said, *see? I can love other humans, so watch out!*

Darrow and Paige had commandeered another chair and sat together. Her belly bulged a bit more than Kate's. She'd deliver around the holidays.

Raze and Elisa were putting the final touches on the decorations around the cake Rylee had carefully placed on a table earlier. She'd had to go pick up Gunner and Josh after that.

Elisa and Raze had volunteered to organize the event even though they were guests like everyone else. I'd caught them making out against the counter, and I understood why. It was a magical counter, one made for love.

"Sorry we're late," Gunner bellowed as he and Rylee stepped through the front door. "Don't open any presents yet because we want you to open ours first." He placed a brightly wrapped package with the others near Kate's chair.

Josh, their young son, raced over to the table where we'd placed the two teddy bears we'd won at the fair. He grabbed them and gave them a hug.

"I can't wait to see what you got," Violet cried, leaning into Goreg's embrace. They stood in the opening to the kitchen. "I'm going to the fridge. Who wants a soda?"

A few called out, and she bustled into the kitchen to fetch them.

Her little sister, Halle, scooted over to Josh, and they raced to the toy box I'd placed in the corner of the room, finding a game and running to the kitchen to set it up on the table to play.

"When should we hold *your* shower?" Vrok asked, coming up behind me. He wrapped himself around me, his big hands stroking my still-flat belly.

"That's not up to me." I scrunched my nose at him. "A pregnant lady doesn't organize her own shower."

"I'm going to do it," Kate said with a grin. "Before I pop these two out, I'm all over it."

She wasn't having triplets, but she *was* having twins. I couldn't wait to snuggle them, and Kate had promised they'd call me auntie.

"Oh no," Nyxor bellowed, rising from where he sat on one end of the sofa. He peered around. "Where is she?"

I'd yet to figure out what he meant when he said that, and I wasn't sure if it was polite to ask.

A poof, and he burst into flames.

Only one person cried out—Nyxor's date. The rest of us had gotten used to him cycling through his phoenix, as he called it.

"I am done with this," his date bellowed. Her scowl took in all of us. "Why aren't all of you doing something to stop this? He's a freak, that's what he is, and I'm done with it." She stormed toward the door. "Tell him *not* to call me again."

The front door banged closed behind her.

Ass. Nyxor was the sweetest guy. He was better off without her.

Gunner brought over a blanket, draping it over where Nyxor had been.

In seconds, Nyxor reappeared beneath the blanket as a phoenix. After one squawk, he morphed back into his gorgeous, manly self.

"Where's Annie?" he asked, looking around.

"She left," Gunner said, rubbing Nyxor's shoulder. "Sorry, man."

With a sad sigh, Nyxor wrapped the blanket around his hips and left the room. The back door opened, and he stepped outside.

"I'll go talk to him," I told Vrok, feeling bad for our friend. None of us mocked him for something he couldn't control, but we all felt sad because *he* did.

"He'd rather you didn't," Vrok said, giving me a hug. "He's told me that he just wants to be alone after it happens."

Aw.

"I imagine he'll sit on the back step and visit with Merith for a bit," he said. "I'll go get him soon. He won't want to miss much of the party."

"Maybe he'll go next door to visit with Brooke," I said, though I didn't think they'd met yet. She was cute, single, and she'd mentioned something about how much she loved living in a town full of monsters. They would get along great. I'd invited her to come over tonight, but she told me she had things she'd kept putting off that needed to be done.

Vrok kissed my cheek, and I sighed, leaning back in his embrace.

"Love you," he whispered.

"Love you too," I said. There was no place better than being in his arms. Our friends surrounded us. Laughter rang out. You could feel the happiness and love in the air.

We'd found our peace about our mate bond, and

since we were thrilled to be together, we'd decided to close that chapter of our life and begin a new one.

All that mattered was me and him and our love for each other.

Could our lives get any better?

My wrists started tingling.

I gasped, and the sound was echoed by Vrok.

We lifted our linked hands, watching as the glorious, wonderful, amazing mate bond symbols reappeared on our skin.

I hope you enjoyed Seyla & Vrok's story!
Next up is Hold Me Closer, Fiery Phoenix,
Brooke & Nyxor's romance.
Will Nyxor & Brooke's quickie wedding
end just as fast in divorce, or will they
find their happy ever after?

Would you like to read the book Seyla is
"working on" (ha ha)?
A Monster Worth Fighting For

Have you checked out the rest of the Monsterville world?

Candy For My Orc Boss, Max & Chastity
Orc Me Baby One More Time, Gunner & Rylee
Gargoyles Just Want to Have Fun, Goreg & Violet
Don't Go Knotting My Heart, Storm & Luna

Whose Bed Have Your Claws Been Under?, Darrow &
Paige
Uptown Ogre, Raze & Elisa
My Orc-y Breaky Heart, Vrok & Seyla
Hold Me Closer, Fiery Phoenix, Nyxor & Brooke
& Who Let the Demon Out?
(Venom & Ali's story)

Would you like a FREE book?
Sign up for my newsletter, and
I'll send you Escorting the Alien,
a complete, HEA romance.

ABOUT THE AUTHOR

Ava Ross is a two-time *USA Today* Bestselling author who has written numerous titles, all of them featuring sweet and steamy romance. She fell for men with unusual features when she first watched Star Wars, where alien creatures have gone mainstream. She lives in New England with her husband (who is sadly not an alien, though he is still cute in his own way), her kids, and a few assorted pets.

SERIES BY AVA

Mail-Order Brides of Crakair

Brides of Driegon

Fated Mates of the Ferlaern Warriors

Fated Mates of the Xilan Warriors

Holiday with a Cu'zod Warrior

Galaxy Games

*Alien Warrior Abandoned/
Shattered Galaxies*

Beastly Alien Boss

Bride of the Fae

A Sci-Fi Holiday Tail

Monsterville, USA

Monster on Board
(co-written with Alana Khan)

A Monster Worth Fighting For
(Monster Between the Sheets)

Love at First Orc

Third Galaxy on the Left

Monster Mate Hunt

You can find my books on Amazon.

HOLD ME CLOSER, FIERY PHOENIX

If I don't find my true love soon, I'll die.

The dating scene can be tough for a phoenix, especially when I burn to cinders at the most inconvenient times. It's gotten to the point where no one will even go out with me.

Worse, my spontaneous combustions are accelerating. I've been cursed with a rare phoenix abnormality and my time's ticking away. Soon, my pile of ashes will be swept up in the wind, and I'll no longer rejuvenate as a phoenix.

Unless I can find my fated mate and convince her to love me.

When the town's dating service, Monster Mingle, offers me a mail-order bride, I agree out of desperation.

I'm married at first sight to Brooke, a woman I haven't seen since we were sixteen, back when her older brother caught us making out and stole her away.

We pick up where we left off, and with the help of my monster friends, I set out to show her I'm the phoenix of her dreams.

Can I convince her to love me before it's too late?

Hold Me Closer, Fiery Phoenix, Book 9 in the Monsterville, USA Series, is a spicy monster romcom. Each book is standalone and best if read in order (see below). Expect romantic hijinks with monsters, heat, and a happily ever after.

Check out the entire Monsterville world!
Candy for my Orc Boss
Orc Me Baby One More Time
Gargoyles Just Want to Have Fun
Don't Go Knotting My Heart
Whose Bed Have Your Claws Been Under?
Uptown Ogre
Oops, I Elf'd it Again
My Orc-y Breaky Heart
Hold Me Closer, Fiery Phoenix
Who Let the Demon Out?
Get Hold Me Closer, Fiery Phoenix Now!

CHAPTER 1
NYXOR

After spontaneously combusting, morphing back into my interim phoenix form, then popping into my mostly human-shape—buck naked—I stepped out of my friend Vrok's house for some fresh air.

Inside, the party continued. A friend, Kate, and her mate, Tylik, were being honored with a baby shower. As much as I'd love to be with them right now, I needed time to think.

Dropping onto Vrok's back steps, I hung out with his pet dragonette, Merith, wishing I could hold back my looming death. I'd recently discovered I was a rivest phoenix. If I didn't find my fated mate and convince her to love me, my phoenix metamorphosis would accelerate until, one of these times, I burned without regeneration.

"Help, help!" someone cried from the other side of the fence between Vrok's place and his neighbor. "Please help!"

The desperation and fear in the voice sent me bolting

off the deck. I tripped over the blanket I'd wrapped around my waist when I rejuvenated without clothing and nearly fell.

I leapt toward the fence. My blanket snagged on something, but I didn't stop to free it. Someone was in grave danger, and who cared if I was naked when I faced it?

My wings extended, I flew over the fence, landing squarely in the middle of the neighbor's backyard.

Darkness had fallen, but I could still make out a woman standing in the grass, wringing her hands.

"What's wrong?" I asked.

Her curly blonde hair bounced across her shoulders as she turned my way, and for one second, she looked familiar. Her curvaceous shape didn't spark my memory, however.

Her dark eyes did.

"Brooke?" The name was wrenched out of me.

She blinked slowly, her head tilting. "Nyxor Thaarn?" Her eyes widened. "Oh, wow, it is you. Nyxor!" She stepped forward, her arms extended, but froze when she got a good look at me. "You're naked." When her eyes glided down my body, stopping at my cock before flashing back up to my face, color flooded her pretty cheeks. "Very naked."

"It's good to see you, Brooke." The last time I'd seen her, we were both sixteen and her brother, Jarrod, caught us making out and dragged her away. I never saw her again, though I'd looked for her.

She was my dream twelve years ago, and I hadn't forgotten her since.

"You too, Nyxor." She sucked in a breath and shot it back out. "I want to catch up, but I can't right now. Twinkie got away, and I can't find him." Her head snapped in all directions. "Twinkie. Twinkie!"

"What's a twinkie?" I asked, internally shouting at my cock to behave. It ignored me, slowly rising toward my abs.

"Twinkie's my new kitten." She peered around. "I picked him up at the shelter a week ago. He got out when I was letting the bird out of my house."

"Bird?" I looked around, looking for a small cat.

"Somehow, a bird got inside. Twinkie, of course, was thrilled, and he chased the poor bird around, leaping, trying to catch it. I carefully moved the bird into the back hall, closing doors, then opened the one on the deck. The bird flew out, but Twinkie followed. I thought he was blocked in the living room." Her face cratered. "Twinkie. Twinkie! Where are you, little fluff ball?"

Movement in the only tree in the backyard drew my eye, and I spied the escapee perched on a branch halfway up the tree.

"Is that your pet?" I asked, pointing.

Her breath caught, and she rushed over to the tree, peering up. "It's him. How did you get up there, little guy?"

"I'll get him down for you." I took wing, soaring upward.

The kitten scrambled back on the branch, nearly

falling off, but I scooped him up and held him against my chest as I flew back to the ground. He clung to my neck, starting to purr.

"Thank you so much," she said as I handed him to her. She held Twinkie snugly in her arms. Her little pet blinked at me, reaching out with a paw as if it thought I was a big bird worth catching.

"You're welcome." I couldn't get over it. After twelve long years, I'd finally met up with Brooke again.

"Why are you naked, Nyxor?" she asked. Laughter bubbled in her voice. "If you're doing something creepy, I might have to call the sheriff."

I tugged my wings around me to cover myself. "Please don't. Demons can be snarly about stuff like this." I placed my palm on my chest. "I promise. I'm not doing anything creepy."

"That doesn't explain your lack of clothing."

"I had a little issue with the blanket I was wearing."

"Blanket?"

"It's a long story." Or a short one in my case. My inner clock was ticking, and soon, I'd explode. "What happened to you back then?" I asked. "You were there and then you weren't."

"I . . ." Her gaze darted away from mine. "I had to leave."

"I'm sorry."

She sighed and stroked Twinkie, who I noted now was a short-haired calico. "Me too. But here you are and here I am. It's wonderful to see a friend again."

"I'm a monster, Brooke. You need to know that." Back then, I used a spell to hide my wings.

Her lips quirked up. "You look like a cute guy to me."

Cute? I liked that. Long ago, I would've collapsed on the ground in joy if she told me she thought I was cute.

"What kind of monster?"

"A phoenix."

"Oh, cool. Wait." A frown appeared on her pretty brow. "How did we meet up twelve years ago if you're a phoenix? Monsters were still hidden."

I scrunched my shoulders. "I kinda snuck through the fae veil."

"No," she breathed, her fingers teasing her lips.

"I moved here once the treaty was finalized," I said. "I'm a lawyer specializing in monster-human contracts. As for why I came outside naked, I was taking a break on my friend's back deck when I heard your call." I didn't want to weigh down our first meet-up with my metamorphosis issues. "I didn't take time to dress."

"I can't believe you were sitting outside with nothing on." She leaned around me, looking toward the fence. "Were you visiting Vrok and Seyla? They're hosting a baby shower tonight. If I'd known you'd show up naked, I might've taken them up on their invitation." Her laugh rang out.

"I guess I should go get dressed." I couldn't hold back the tease in my voice. "If you decide to stop by the shower—and strip to join in on the fun—let me know, because I'll be happy to meet you at the front door."

Like a superhero, I flapped my wings, lifting off and flying over the fence. Running, but oh well.

"Wait," she shouted after me. "I don't have your number!"

***

The next afternoon, I drove into town for my appointment with Monster Mingle, the local matchmaking service. The bell overhead jangled as I entered the office, and I paused in the open reception area.

"Welcome," Grannie Vi said cheerfully where she sat knitting in a rocking chair parked in front of the big picture window overlooking Main Street. She wore an old-fashioned gown and a ruffled cap on her head, and the rocker creak-creak-creaked from her movements.

Uncle Bub sat beside her in a matching rocker, also knitting, though he'd opted to dress as if he was ready to step onto the set of a wild west movie in scuffed jeans, a button up shirt and a worn leather vest with a star sheriff's badge. He'd somehow grown a handlebar moustache, something he was missing when I saw him last week. It must be fake, glued in place.

"What are you doing?" I asked them both.

Grannie's gray eyebrows lifted. "Knitting."

"I could tell, but what are you making?"

"Well, see, business here isn't as steady as we'd like, so we're keeping busy."

"I'm sorry."

"It's okay. Since Bub and I plan to elope soon, we'll

shut down and by the time we return after our Bali wedding, monsters and humans will be lining up for our services." She held up what she was working on. "Baby booties for Kate and Tylik's new baby. I'll make a second pair since they're having twins."

"My Vi is wise, isn't she?" Bub asked, his knitting needles clicking together.

"I thought green would work for them both," she said. "Since they don't know what they're having."

"That's my Vi," Uncle Bub said. "Sharper than one of Gunner's hand-hewn swords."

Gunner, the town's orc blacksmith, also crafted weapons and metal sculptures.

Bub held his work up. "I'm making scarves for the homeless. After I've made a hundred, I'm gonna start knitting sweaters."

"That's amazing," I said. "Back to what you just said, Grannie." I couldn't believe my ears. "You two are eloping? What does Rylee have to say about that?" Vi's granddaughter, Rylee, was married to Gunner and she owned a cupcake shop here in town.

Grannie's rocker came to a halt, and she leveled me a heavy stare. "Why would I need to consult Rylee about this?"

"Because she'll want to hold a big event for you. Wouldn't Raze and Elisa want to organize it? It would be the biggest and most amazing wedding this town has ever seen." I wasn't joking. Everyone loved Grannie Vi and Uncle Bub.

Grannie Vi wasn't my grandmother, and Uncle Bub

wasn't my uncle. Everyone in town just called them that. Vi had moved to Monsterville with Rylee, and she and Bub had hit it off from the start. Bub had moved here with his niece, Violet, and he lived with her and her husband, a gargoyle named Goreg, at their B&B.

Except now they were marrying. Had they moved in together?

"I supposed we could consider having a big shindig here," Grannie Vi said, starting her rocker and her knitting again. "What do you think, Bub? I'd look amazing in a white lace gown, and you could wear a white suit with a red bow tie."

Uncle Bub beamed. "That sounds dandy, Vi. Are you sure you don't want a destination wedding in Bali?"

She shrugged. "I imagine it's hot there this time of year, and you know my unmentionable areas get irritated when they're sweaty."

"Mine, too, Vi," he said with a chuckle. "Mine too." His gaze met mine. "A&D ointment, son. That's the trick. Make sure you put on a generous layer."

"I'll write that down," I said, trying not to laugh.

"Nyxor has the right idea," Vi said. "We'll hold a huge wedding and invite everyone in town. You'll come, won't you, Nyxor?"

"Of course." I grinned. There wasn't anything I'd rather do than witness their marriage.

"You'll need a date, naturally," she said, her eyes taking on an odd slant. Mischief? Nah. She was a sweet old lady, not someone who'd manipulate others when they weren't looking. "It's a good thing you're here."

"I have an appointment."

"See? Perfect."

"You've got a match for me?"

"Even better than that," she said.

Bub grinned, showing off his pearly white dentures. "Remember how you indicated you were open to our newfangled idea?"

I frowned. They'd mentioned lots of ideas after my third dating failure. "Which one is that?"

"We've hooked you up with a mail-order bride."

I gulped. "Bride?"

"You did state you were open to a trial relationship if we could find your ideal match."

"Yer in luck, my boy," Bub cried. "We let the computer do the work for us, and she'll be here to meet you soon."

"I'm not opposed to getting married, but you know my track record with dating. I can't talk to anyone into going out with me more than once." Dating had given me multiple chances to meet women and find my fated mate. Once we'd met and fallen in love, I'd be able to control my phoenix blaze. With time running out, though, I wasn't sure I wanted to marry someone who wasn't the right one.

Grannie dropped her knitting onto a nearby table and rose, grabbing her cane, using it to approach me. "Why don't you come back to the office with me? We can wait there until she arrives."

"Hold on," I said as she grabbed my arm and tugged

me down the hall. "How did you find someone willing to marry me so quickly?"

"We tracked her down in an online chat group, of course." She urged me into her office and pushed me down into a chair. "We figured if we hooked you up with someone willing to marry you sight unseen, your odds of bliss would improve greatly." Her gaze took in my jeans and flannel shirt. "You're not dressed well enough for your wedding, but we have a plan for that."

When I started to rise, she pressed me back into the chair. I could set her aside easily, but there was no way I'd do anything to hurt an old lady.

"I'll sit on you if you don't stay still," she said, shaking her finger in my face. "Behave."

"Alright," I said, holding up my hands. "I'll meet her." There was no harm in that. If she wasn't the right one, I could back out before saying I do.

I was running out of options after my date bailed on me at Kate's baby shower. If I didn't find my fated one soon and convince her to love me, my spontaneous combustions would accelerate until I was consumed one final time, never to reappear as a phoenix again.

Of course, I couldn't stop thinking about Brooke. But for all I knew, she was already married.

With a toothy grin, Grannie rounded the desk to take her chair.

The bell jangled as someone opened the front door, but while whoever it was spoke, I couldn't understand what they said.

Bub's cane rang out in the hall. "Right this way. Right

this way. Your future husband is waiting." He appeared in the doorway. "And here he is."

Brooke poked her head around him, her eyes widening when she saw me.

Get Hold Me Closer, Fiery Phoenix Now!